ROCKSTAR SINNERS

FORBIDDEN CHORDS SERIES

JA'NESE DIXON

PUBLISHING

This is a work of fiction. All of the characters, organization and events portrayed in this story are either products of the author's imagination or are used fictitiously.

For more information address:

Purpose Prevails Publishing
2231B Center St. STE 144
Deer Park, TX 77536
www.purposeprevailspublishing.com

Forbidden Chords Series (Contemporary Romance)

Rockstar Secrets (Book 1)

Rockstar Sinners (Book 2)

Rockstar Billionaire (Book 3) (*Coming soon*)

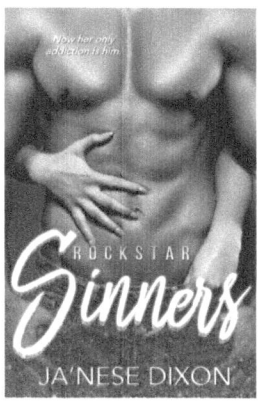

Can she convince him that her only addiction is him?

Sydney "Lady Bird" Jones took sex, drugs, and rock 'n roll to the extreme—literally—until she woke up determined to put the limelight in her rearview mirror.

Cameron Carter can spot raw talent a mile away with his eyes closed and ears plugged. He stumbles into a small Austin showcase, and the songstress captures his attention and his heart.

Sydney believes the sexy executive belongs in her bed as Cameron fights to maintain professional boundaries against the need to possess every inch of her. But when a demon comes to haunt her, he might as well sign his death certificate.

CHAPTER ONE

*T*he Bat City had officially driven him batshit crazy. Cameron Carter wanted to glue his eyes shut and stuff his ears with cotton. He wasn't prone to theatrics. But layering his desire to build Rockstar Entertainment with a demanding travel schedule turned cool, calm Cameron into an agitated and prickly version of himself.

He groaned rubbing a hand over his face as his head fell back to the cool leather headrest. His eyes slid closed as he scanned his memory of the people and music he experienced the past ten days at South by Southwest in Austin. None of them would do.

Now, all he wanted was to drive back to Houston to sleep in his own bed. But he told the guys he'd meet them at Smith & Jameson tonight. And Cameron's word was his bond. His Pops taught him that.

As one of the five partners with Rockstar Entertainment, Cameron's role as the leader of their unconventional bunch meant he managed their business affairs *and* he found the talent. They finally launched their flagship artist, Marques Carter, and RSE was ready to sign new talent starting tonight. They were surprising one of their staff musicians, Isaac Jones, with a production deal. So, he guessed the trip wasn't a total wash. Isaac deserved this shot. But Cameron went to Austin looking for one thing. A queen for RSE.

Marques went from the Prince of R&B to the King in a sea of trap music and hip-hop. And every king needed a queen.

So, his trip was split between attending the daytime sessions to make connections with other music executives and his nights club hopping. He went from venue to venue, night after night, searching for a gem in the midst of rubble with no luck.

Giving Isaac this contract would be the highlight of his trip because he failed to find what he was looking for. Granted, he didn't want just *any* artist. After their success with Marques, Cameron wanted the female version to embody the sound and heart of RSE. Her sexy had to match their swag.

Rough, yet soft. Sultry, but real. Relevant and soulful.

And she had to *sang*! Not sing, not hum, not whine. She had to make the hairs on the back of his neck give a standing ovation. He'd settle for nothing less.

He couldn't. All eyes were on RSE to see if they could produce another star. And it all started with Cameron. But only if he could find *her*.

Cameron sat in the same spot for almost a half hour

willing his body to move. He opened his eyes and glanced at the restaurant across the street then to the digital clock on the dashboard. He had a couple hours before the scheduled gathering with the guys. That would give him enough time to catch up with Asher and Dylan, the owners of Smith & Jameson—a couple of old friends.

Cameron needed to get moving. Since he was in town, they needed him to check on the arrangements. Isaac thought they were coming down to hang out for his birthday. They reserved the VIP suite and planned to pop a few bottles. The entire team would be on deck to watch Isaac ink his deal.

He reached for the door handled, climbing out of the car. He crossed the street gathering his resolve to endure yet another copycat artist on another stage because this was Austin, the live music capital of the world.

The sheer volume of artists with the same sound, same lyrical content about cars and women and money wore him out. Cameron was over it nine days ago. Yet here he was walking into another establishment. After tonight, he didn't want to hear another note from another soul for at least a month. But he had a soundtrack to score.

Cameron reached for the door and entered S&J. Asher and Dylan opened it a couple years ago, and this was his first visit. The placed looked packed.

He stood in line behind a few people as they inched their way to the hostess. His eyes slowly swept the room. Beautiful dark wood ran the length of the interior. The waiting area had stain-glass walls on either side. Soft music played over the speakers.

Cameron took a deep breath, the mellow, grown and sexy vibe brought a smile to his face. He could feel the tension in his neck relaxing as he stepped forward.

"Well, well, well, if it isn't the man himself." Cameron turned towards the sound of Asher Smith. A smile crossed Asher's face, a face that hadn't changed since college.

"The man? Naw, you *the man*." They gripped hands, leaning in for a one-armed hug. Then they pulled back to look out over the restaurant. Cameron was impressed. "Look at this place."

"Thanks. We are truly blessed. Let me give you a quick tour before I show you to the VIP suite." Asher motioned him inside, and Cameron followed, walking past the hostess.

"You can see the bar here," Asher motioned to the far wall, "and back there is where we have your gathering set up."

Cameron nodded. The bar held the same dark wood with a mirrored wall behind it.

"That area is the lounge." They walked to a doorway, the room held a small stage with instruments. "We have live music tonight."

Cameron couldn't suppress his groan.

"Nah man." Asher laughed, stepping closer to let a couple walk around them. "It's Isaac and his band."

"Oh, word?"

Asher nodded. Cameron glanced at his watch. This

night was looking up. He planned to drive back to Houston but listening to Isaac's set may chase away the memories of the autotune, half-naked presentations he'd witnessed all week.

"I'll have to hang around after our celebration."

"You don't have to hang around. They are scheduled to start in about thirty minutes. How about this?" Asher gripped his shoulder and pointed to a set of glass doors. "Head out those doors to the courtyard and grab some food. I'll get you a table set up in here. We can catch up and listen to them play before you head back to your suite."

"I'd like that." And Cameron meant it. He could smell the food already. He could hear them play, hang with his family, then head home tonight. Yes, this night was looking up indeed.

"Bet."

Asher headed in one direction, and Cameron went in the other. They didn't visit each other often, but they talked by phone frequently. Asher and Dylan worked hard to get S&J open and judging by the crowd inside, the people of Austin appreciated their efforts.

Cameron let his nose lead the way as he loosened his tie. His suit and tie made him appear overdressed compared to the casual attire of the other patrons. He removed his jacket and draped it over his forearm as he reached the glass doors.

But the scent of warm honey stopped him in his tracks. Cameron froze and glanced from side to side. The soft fragrance canceled out the aroma of barbecue and the spice of Thai. And his eyes locked with who he presumed was the culprit. His heartbeat dropped to a sultry crawl as her eyes boldly scanned him. He turned in her direction intending to give her a full display.

Her light brown skin and full curly hair made her stand out in the dimly lit room. Her sinful curves were the ones songs were made of. A delicate hand draped on her hip with a body-hugging dress that fell to the floor in a puddle of black sequin.

The flames in her eyes were bright enough to cut through the room and ignite a trail of heated sensation across his skin. It took every drop of resolve to remain put. She looked like the red carpet type. The kind of woman ready to stand in the spotlight. The type of woman he'd take to fancy industry parties and travel around the world. And those weren't usually the marrying type.

Okay, maybe he didn't want the marrying type just yet. But there was no way he could sample her and live to tell the tale.

Cameron commanded his feet to move and let another man succumb to her alluring gaze. Because giving in to what his body wanted right now would be asking for trouble. And he'd learned the hard way that women like the honey-dipped beauty standing less than ten feet away tend to be trouble with all capital letters.

Trouble that he couldn't afford. Especially since he'd been asked to oversee the score for a major motion picture, thanks to his cousin. So, the pressure to assemble the RSE roster was amplified by one thousand percent. He had a label to build. Artists to sign. Music to record.

Cameron tipped his head, and her ruby red lips parted into a smile showing beautiful white teeth. His chest felt tight. Was the universe serious right now?

Keep your eyes on the prize. He pushed open the heavy glass door and found himself in the open courtyard.

Cameron had one "real" relationships, and it managed to annihilate his heart with a sledgehammer. Then he witnessed Marques' wedding and his love for his wife, Brione. Something inside Cameron shifted. And he no longer wanted to be known as *Playboy Carter*.

That reality and Cameron's nonstop schedule had him spending his nights alone. Not due to the lack of offerings. However, in his position, gorgeous women were the norm. Cameron attended the "it" parties, red carpet premiers, exclusive events. They all wanted to be wined and dined and pampered. They all wanted to be seen on his arm. They all wanted something.

Cameron, the music executive. Cameron, the son of a celebrity. Cameron, the mogul. None of them wanted Cameron, the man.

He'd played along because they all knew the deal. It worked, for a while.

He circled the globe. He sampled its offerings. Cameron was a fisher of *wo*men, having his fun. But his big houses were empty. And a part of him was ready to settle down.

Cameron had played and lost at love. He wasn't a

quitter, but he wasn't glutton for punishment either. He glanced back at the door.

He wanted to ask her name. Did she have a man? Did she *want* a man? But none of that was his business. To get something different, he had to *be* someone different. And she looked to be more of the same. A party girl, looking for a good time.

He'd learned the more success they saw with RSE that catching a woman wasn't the issue. Catching the *right* woman was.

A woman not hypnotized by it all. A woman not "enthralled by the glitz and glamour of fame," as his Pops liked to put it.

Cameron walked towards the food trucks. Space would do him well. But her warm honey scent left a lasting impression.

And on everything, he wasn't ready to expose his heart not when casually dating gave him the freedom of keeping it stored away for safekeeping. Opening himself up meant letting someone in. *Again*.

It was best to focus on the task at hand. Nail the soundtrack. Forget the girl. Nah, wasn't nothing girl in her, she was all woman.

Forget the woman, focus on the music.

Tonight he'd enjoy his family and friends. Then back to business.

"Cameron?"

He glanced over his shoulder as Isaac closed the space between them. "Hey man."

"You good?"

"Yeah man, what's up?"

"I called you a few times."

"Man, my head is stuffed with this week's ratchet music. I need a vacation to cleanse my music palette."

They laughed as they walked closer to the food trucks. Cameron was still shook by her ruby red lips and sexy full hips. He honestly hadn't heard Isaac.

"Well, you're in for a treat tonight."

"A treat?" He turned towards Isaac.

"Yes, sir. My sister decided to join us tonight for the first set. I had to beg her." He laughed.

"Beg?" Cameron scanned the signs trying to decide on what to eat. He settled on the barbecue.

"Beg, *and* I promised to take her shopping at the Galleria Mall in Houston."

"Oh dang!" Cameron ran his hand over his fade. "You better dust off your credit card."

Isaac covered his mouth as he laughed. "Tell me about it. But it's worth it. You'll see."

"Let me grab some food and then hear this black-mailing sister of yours."

"Alright, cool. And thanks for coming."

"No doubt. You're family." They hugged, and Cameron watched as Isaac went back inside. Tonight would be an excellent night for RSE. Isaac was a gifted young musician and a valuable member of RSE's house band. But pairing him with Bruce could groom him to be an amazing artist.

Cameron moved forward and ordered a sausage sandwich then hurried back inside. He shook his head at the thought of Isaac's sister squeezing her brother for a shopping spree. It sounded like his little sister Lauren.

Cameron made it back to the lounge. He searched the room, and Asher flagged him down. He approached the table surprised by the sight. The Smith tribe was in full effect.

"Mrs. Smith?" He placed his plate on the table.

"It's Mrs. Reinheart." She still looked more like Asher's sister, and not a day over thirty. Cameron chuckled at the hell they gave Asher in college over his mother. All the guys wanted a shot.

"I guess I missed my chance." Cameron wiggled his eyebrows jokingly.

"Boy please." Asher's mother stood and hugged him.

"And don't hug my wife too tight."

Cameron outright laughed. "Nah man. I wouldn't dare."

"Jaxon, I'm with her." He kissed her then extended a hand.

"Cameron." Jaxon looked to be their age. *Go 'head Mrs. Reinheart.*

"But I don't blame you. She is *fine*." Jaxon slipped in before circling an arm around his wife.

Cameron laughed. "No comment."

"You better not. Always drooling over my moms. You *know* I'll hurt you over my momma!" Asher added. Cameron decided to keep his lips sealed. Asher's mother was always fine, still was. "You met her husband. I'd like to introduce you to my wife, Jazz."

They hugged. "Nice to meet you."

"And you know this guy. He finally married my sister." Asher elbowed Dylan.

"Yuki," Cameron grabbed his heart as if she wounded him, "don't tell me I missed my shot with you too."

"Dude, you acting real thirsty right now," Dylan added pulling Cameron into a hug.

"Can you blame me? All these beautiful women." Cameron shook his hands for emphasis, taking the free seat beside Asher.

"Yes, I can blame you. Get your own woman." Dylan said.

"Oh no, not *Playboy Carter*." Asher teased.

They laughed. Their energy and love were infectious. The Smiths rivaled the Carters as they all talked over one another, completed each other's sentences, and he laughed until he cried. He sat back in the seat and took a long drink of the cold beer. Adding in a word or two as the women allowed. He passed a few pictures of his own, showcasing his beautiful niece.

They caught him up on the growth of their family, passing around cellphones full of pictures. He was truly happy for his friends.

Cameron finally bit into his sandwich. He groaned to his core.

"It's good ain't it?" Asher smiled.

"Man!" He wiped the smoky sauce from his mouth. This singer could sound like a toad and Cameron wouldn't care. His outlook on the night went from gloom to promising. Good food. Great friends. Sitting back listening to them made this trip worth it.

Then the lights dimmed. Asher's wife started clapping and bouncing up and down in her chair before the music began.

"My Lady, she hasn't even started," Asher whispered, the love in his voice made Cameron glance over.

"You know she's my favorite." Jazz whispered back.

"Y'all hush," Yuki added from across the table, settling into Dylan's side.

Cameron figured he had about a year to pull off this soundtrack. A year to assemble a formidable roster of artists to present their sound to the world. He wanted all the tracks to feature RSE artists. But the look they shared paled in comparison to the success he sought. It was one he envied. And like Marques and Brione, they all gave him hope. He lifted the sandwich entertained by their banter until he heard her first note.

*N*ervous jitters swirled in her stomach as Sydney Jones stepped to the microphone. And the feeling never ever got old. It was sort of like real life magic. Fairy tales and birthday cake. And everything that makes life worth living. But it almost killed her.

Not metaphorically. But a real stretched out on a gurney, rushed to the emergency room, death situation. And all because of her first and only love, music. She took the whole, sex, drugs, and rock n' roll to the extreme. Not the sex, but the drugs and touring, pushing her body to limit until she nearly overdosed.

"The pieces of me, are like ashes in the wind…."

Sydney closed her eyes as her first public notes in five years emerged from the pit of her soul, bubbling up to the service. She requested the low house lights to conceal her nerves and to mute the accessing eyes. Most people heard about her overdose. It was the worse day of her life, but tonight she would sing for her brother Isaac and walk away again. *She had to.*

She settled in for the set. Letting the music be the escape it once was. Isaac and his band backed her every note, scat, and adlib. Opening her eyes, she glanced at him, the euphoria was written on his face, and she couldn't contain her joy.

Was it possible to love the very thing that was detrimental to her health? Her very life?

Yes.

Sydney scanned the room, feeding off the energy of the audience as heads bobbed, and fingers snapped. A woman near the stage sat with a pained expression on her face. That was music too. It could take you back to a place, a time, a love.

The next notes Sydney dug deeper and let voice intentionally crack. To make it ache. To make it tell a story. Her story. Their story.

The final note escaped in a whisper, and she stepped back into the shadows of the stage. She could probably hear a pin drop, and then a thunderous sound filled the room as they clapped and cheered.

Sydney held back tears.

"Thank you." She used the black towel on the bar stool to dab her eyes. "Tonight is my baby brother's birthday. Can y'all help me out?"

They hooped and hollered.

"On the count of three, let's sing Happy Birthday. One…two…three…."

And as requested, the crowd sang to Isaac, and she

used the time to get herself together. Isaac was the light in her life. He helped piece her back together when everyone turned their backs on her. He didn't give up on her.

"Y'all sound beautiful." She took a drink of water, letting the shadows nurse her tatter soul. As they transitioned from the traditional rendition to the Stevie Wonder version.

"Happy Birthday to ya…"

Sydney held the microphone towards them as the band joined in.

"Give yourselves a round of applause." They clapped louder as Isaac bowed. "I think I can dig up a few more songs if you'd like to hear them."

The overwhelming sound encouraged her to continue. Sydney signaled the band and the music to a mellow Jill Scott number. Man could these guys play.

Sydney stepped back into the spotlight. And the lights shimmered off her sequin mermaid dress. She dropped the drugs and picked up cooking. It gave her a few more pounds than she was used to, but it made the rock of her body solid. A few people stood, as she cooed about living her life like it was golden.

Yeah, music was magical. She rounded the verse out and hit the chorus, and the audience hit every note and queue like real background singers. Sydney laughed tossing her curls back and forth, dancing around the stage. Clapping her hands over her head as the audience bellowed about freedom and she slipped into the moment.

The song ended, and this time they didn't wait. Every man and woman stood on their feet. She clapped along blowing kisses, smiling so hard her face ached.

"We need to take this act on the road." They laughed along with her. And as they took their seats, she wiped the sweat from her face. "Y'all I saw this fine brother tonight."

"Alright now!" A woman yelled.

"Yes, girl. Tall, chocolate and fiiiine." She fluffed her hair and shook her shoulders. That got them laughing again. "He was *so* fine I had to change my set list to add this one." She flicked her wrist toward Isaac. He hit the introductory notes, and the party continued. "Oh y'all know this one too." She gave her sassiest wink and settled the microphone into the stand. "This is what I should have said to him."

Sydney cooed about his brown skin, rolling her hips to the Indie Arie joint that had the women grabbing their men. The silhouettes of couples slow dancing between the tables scattered around the room. She let the words flow like smooth milk chocolate, as she allowed him to run through her mind. And then she spotted him.

Center table near the back. And unlike the rest of the audience, his eyes were locked on her. The intensity pulled her from across the room.

Might as well make it count. Sydney slipped into her sultriest rendition, and the band didn't miss a beat.

Her admirer leaned forward, and she let the words of the song do the talking. His eyes closed for the briefest moment, as his head rolled side to side, so slow she almost missed it. When his eyes opened the look he gave her made her want to jump off the stage.

The song ended, and Isaac thumped on his bass for her final number, and every hand went up in the air. Fingers snapped, bodies rocked.

For her last selection, the lights lowered back to a dim, and she beckoned him to her using the words from Marvin Gaye, Sydney took them on a journey. Crooning for the lover outside her reach.

She sent the message with her body, every calculated wale, and extended note. *Mr. Suit-and-Tie, I'm gonna make you come to me.*

The bridge came, and Isaac took over for the guitar solo. Sydney closed her eyes, letting her hips sway, as the melody from the crowd built in a simmering chant, singing the words of the chorus.

Sydney sprinkled her well-placed runs around the room. Then she took them all up a notch folding over and coming up tossing her hair reaching towards the object of her affection.

Her signature beg and plea blended with riffs of the guitar and the audience brought it on home. The song ended and thunderous sound filled the room again, seeping into her pours, and this was why she loved music. *To bad her love didn't love her.*

Sydney turned towards the band and clapped with the audience. Isaac grabbed her hand, lifting it up and they screamed so loud she thought she'd be deaf. She'd have to soak it up. This was a one time gig.

She mouthed her thanks making eye contact with

people here and there. Then her eyes found his, standing as if a spotlight hung over his head. The expression on his face said he felt every word she sent his way.

"Give it up one more time for my big sister, Sydney "Lady Bird" Jones."

She bowed and exited the stage. *I need a drink.*

WHAT A SHOW! CAMERON HAD TO HAVE HER.

He'd never had an experience like that in his life. The hour set exceeded his expectations. She radiated star quality. She had that elusive "it" factor that can't be trained or explained. It just was. And she had it in abundance.

He was raised in a musical family, and it gave him an advantage. He'd seen his father perform with his group for his entire life. He'd seen his brother perform around the world. But Sydney put a hoax on the audience with each sway of her hips, bounce of her curls, and her voice. *God that voice.* He wanted to experience it again.

Cameron stepped around Asher and made his way to the side door. The audience stood clapping, still transfixed by her show. Thankful for his six foot, one-inch height, he bobbed and weaved through the crowd, extending his neck to see which way she went. His heart raced faster than his feet could carry him. He crossed the doorway, and he ran smack dab into Bruce Daniels, his music man, and partner with RSE.

"Man, I was coming in to find you. Everyone is waiting for you." Bruce gestured over his shoulder.

"Did you see a woman in a black dress come through here?" Cameron used his hands to cast her silhouette while scanning the length of the walkway in search of her curly fro. He guesstimated she stood to his shoulder. But her hair should make it easy to spot her. He saw nothing.

Bruce shook his head. "What woman?"

"Isaac's sister." He walked toward the front, she disappeared. The people were flowing out of the lounge, and it buzzed with energy.

"Isaac's sister?"

"Yeah, man. Isaac's sister. Sydney *something* Jones." He was getting agitated with all the questions as the area between the lounge and bar flooded with people. They swirled around him obstructing his view.

"You mean, Sydney "Lady Bird" Jones?" Bruce spoke over the crowd.

Cameron stopped turning back to Bruce, zeroing in on his best friend, and business partner. "You know her?"

"And you don't?"

"Should I?" Cameron wanted to scrub the humor off Bruce's face. But not knowing most artists helped him form an independent opinion based on the music. It let the music, be the music.

"And she's here?" He heard the awe in Bruce's voice, as they scanned the swelling crowd for her.

"Yes. She. Is. *Here.* " He glanced back inside the lounge. "She *was* here."

"And I missed it?"

"Bruce." Cameron stopped in front of him. The adrenaline from the show and his desire to find his curvy bombshell had him ready to throttle Bruce. "*Who is she*?"

"Cam, I don't know if you want to entertain that one. She has an amazing voice. But I'm not sure she's what you're looking for." He averted Cameron's gaze.

"I need her for the soundtrack. Her show was electric. The audience loved her. You should have seen it. Fast. Slow. She didn't miss a beat. When we put her voice with your music…. We'd be unstoppable."

Sydney was the queen he needed for RSE. All that sexiness hypnotized the entire audience, him included. And she had the chops to back it up.

"She is a star, man, I know it." Cameron paced in a circle collecting his thoughts. "It was like throwing Whitney, Lauren, Amy, and Mary J into a crock pot. That woman was *bad*. I want her Bruce."

Cameron found them. Bruce molded them. It was a team effort.

He could see it now. Never mind knowing she flicked on every switch in his body. He couldn't have her, have her. Not in his bed. Not sample those full lips. Not if he wanted her as an artist.

He had a feeling those ruby lips would haunt him.

"Want who?"

Cameron looked up to see his brother, Marques, and the whole team standing beside him—Devin, Jamal, and Damian. Having all the partners in town meant they could vote tonight.

Cameron led the team, but they had a policy of

needing 100% agreement when signing an artist. But Cameron made the final call. He could hear her voice over Bruce's tracks. He would have Marques write a few songs for her.

He turned to explain and heard Isaac walk up. "Which way did you sister go?"

Isaac blinked a few times as if surprised by Cameron's outburst. "She left."

"What do you mean she left?" Cameron's heart dropped.

"Bars aren't her thing. She came for the first set only."

Cameron ran a hand over his face. "I need you to call her and get her back here. Tonight. I want to sign her to RSE."

THE ADRENALINE FLOODED HER VEINS. IT WAS THE MOST addictive high brought on after singing on stage. Sydney sat in her car taking several deep breaths, gathering her thick hair into a messy bun. She cranked up the air condition leaning closer to the vents and used a towel to dab at the sweat running down her neck.

What a show!

She flipped down the visor and laughed at the mess before her. She'd sweated off her makeup, but her lipstick was intact. The urge to grab a glass of Hennessy and smoke a cigarette made her shift the car into gear. She imagined she'd always associate the stage with her past lifestyle. A lifestyle she no longer wanted for herself.

"Happy Birthday Isaac." She said to the empty car.

Sydney tossed the damp towel in the passenger seat flipping the visor closed. She enjoyed it while it lasted, now it was time to leave S&J and head home. She'd take a cold shower, cook herself a hot meal, and find a way to push Mr. Suit-and-Tie and the ache for music, and the stage, from her mind. This wasn't her life anymore.

CHAPTER THREE

*C*ameron suppressed the urge to run after Sydney. Tonight was all for Isaac. His performance proved what they already knew. He would be a significant asset to RSE and the industry.

The VIP suite held an oversized conference table. The staffed decorated the room with birthday streamers and a cake on a stand in the back of the room. The food lined the far wall in a buffet style with two to three dishes from each of the truck vendors.

S&J had an excellent concept of bridging international ales and international cuisine. Cameron would have to add them to their roster of event locations.

"Surprise!" Clapping brought Cameron back to the matter at hand as Isaac stood in the doorway of the room.

His face filled with shock, scanning the room. RSE chartered a private airplane to fly the entire team to Austin. Cameron walked over to greet the man of the hour.

"What is this?" Isaac said, a slight quiver in his voice.

"We want to show you how much we appreciate your hard work, your endless touring, and your superb musicality."

Isaac dropped his gaze and Cameron grip his neck, much like he handled his younger brothers. Twenty-five was in Cameron's rearview mirror. It would be the beginning for Isaac.

"You came to us wet behind the ears." The crowd laughed, and Isaac did too. He looked up with unshed tears in his eyes. "You have put in the time and the energy. We hope this small token of our appreciation will show just how much we love you, man."

Cameron stepped back giving Isaac some space. "But first we have a question." He took the contract from Damian, "Would you like to become an official member of the RSE family?"

Isaac glanced up and around the semi-circle. Each of the partners stood before him like a hedge of protection, standing in solidarity. Cameron could tell by the slight quiver in his lip, Isaac was about to crack.

"Ladies, will you give us a few minutes. Eliana, I'll need you back in about ten minutes." Cameron waited for the room to clear, leaving the RSE partners. A few squeezed Isaac's shoulder, whispering congratulations as they walked. "We don't want to overwhelm you or pressure you."

"It's not that," Isaac said, brushing away tears. "You don't understand what you're offering me. This contract means the world to me." He reached for it. Still not looking up to meet Cameron's gaze. "Cam you took a chance on me when all I had was a used bass guitar and a dream. I didn't have a cent to my name. I was a kid on my own. And now this."

Isaac's head dropped, and the guys rallied around him.

Cameron gripped the back of his neck and pulled Isaac into a bear hug. "Family…"

"Over fame." The guys finished without hesitation.

"Isaac, you don't need this contract to know that you are family." Cameron watched him mature from a boy rough around the edges to a leader. "You could tell us 'Go to hell,' and we'd still consider you a part of our family and team."

Isaac chuckled. "Nah man. Never." He stood upright and looked around the room. "I'd sign that contract in blood if I had to."

"No blood is needed. But you will work, harder than you ever have." Cameron locked eyes with him, then motioned to the table.

Cameron sat at the head. "This is a formality, but I want you to know how we work before you sign." He used a finger to reinforce his words, tapping on the contract in front of him. "Our motto is 'Family Over Fame' because the men around this table will officially become your big brothers. Invested in your success. Support for when the load seems a little too heavy to bare.

"We want to see you exceed your wildest dreams in this industry but most of all we want to see you thrive as a man." He glanced around the table, this was their legacy.

Cameron gestured to his left to start the proceedings, "Marques Carter is both an artist and a partner. You'll work with him to improve your writing skills and while we're grooming you, you'll serve as his creative director, alongside Brione."

Marques tipped his head, "Welcome to RSE."

"Thanks, man."

"Devin Moore handles marketing, promotion, distribution—"

"I deliver babies, cook a gourmet meal, throw a mean party…" He chuckled, his high voltage smile on deck. The guys laughed. He stood giving Isaac a pound.

"And he's the resident jokester." Cameron laughed. Devin knew how to lighten the mood. "Besides his stellar jokes, you'll shadow him from time-to-time. Don't let the jokes fool ya. This man knows people. He knows music. He knows how to bridge the gap between artistry and album sales." Isaac glanced over at Devin with a new appreciation in his eyes. "You'll quickly learn we support one another. We all wear many hats. We fill in where needed and it's important to know how your music moves from your mind to your fans."

Isaac nodded. Cameron could see the wheels turning, and it pleased him. He'd have to be a quick study to keep up with this bunch.

"Jamal Washington will—"

"Make sure you won't go broke."

"Here here!" Their laughter filled the room as Eliana slipped back into the room.

Jamal was one of the closest to Isaac. He extended a hand. "We'll make sure you're squared away."

"I can't lie about that one. It is true. Jamal is our resident Midas." Cameron paused. "We don't do shady deals. We take care of family. If you follow the path we've established, you'll be a millionaire before you're thirty."

Isaac's eyes tripled in size.

"Yes, let the sink in." The men around him nodded. Most of them were born wealthy, but each had managed to amassed wealth on his own accord too. "You worked with Damian Hughes."

"Yes, he helped me with my house."

Cameron nodded. "Well, this is our resident MacGyver. He's an attorney first. Real estate mogul second. Actually, scratch that. He's a philanthropist first, lawyer, real estate developer. He now heads our legal department around his work with Harmony Dance."

Damian smiled. "I have a few cards for outside counsel. We will cover the cost for you to have your contracts reviewed by anyone of your choice. We stand behind our deals, but you should always have a team you trust to assist you." He slid a folder over to Isaac. "My card is inside too. Use it anytime."

"Thank you." Isaac glanced inside and back at Cameron.

"Last but definitely not least, Bruce Daniels. You know him. But you will probably hate this man when you're done. He will bring out the best in you. Listen to what he says, and you'll surprise even yourself."

"Trust. But don't plan to sleep for the next three years." Marques added.

"How many plaques do you have on your walls?" Bruce asked leaning forward.

"A lot. *Because* you are a slave driver." Marques laughed.

"These two can go at it all night," Cameron cut into their bickering. "You will work primarily with Bruce. This is a production deal. We want to groom you to stand toe-to-toe with these two." Cameron gestured to Bruce and Marques on either side of him.

"As a team, we are committed to developing your sound, your craft, and your legacy. This," he tapped the contract, "is just the beginning."

"But know you'll work hard for it." Bruce sat back. "And we'll help you every step of the way."

Every man nodded. Cameron trusted these men with his life.

"I am offering you this production deal with the 100% agreement of each man at this table. We have a strict moral code of conduct. No drugs, no excessive drinking. We want our artist to be beyond reproach. This is not like other record labels. We don't boast about criminal records and jewelry. Don't get me wrong. We know how to have a good time. But as a member of Rockstar Entertainment, we carry rockstar as a badge of honor. We look towards the future creating music meant to endure a lifetime. And we need *you* to make it happen."

Cameron passed the contract to Isaac while Eliana passed out copies to each of the men. "And I can't forget Eliana Marshall. You've worked with her before too. She knows everything, sees everything, she's the oil that keeps the gears of this machine moving."

Isaac gave a tight nod, and Eliana dropped her gaze taking the seat over his shoulder. Cameron glanced back at her and across the table at Isaac again. *What was that about?*

"Gentlemen, turn to page one."

THEY COVERED THE CONTRACT. PAGE BY PAGE. CLAUSE BY clause. Isaac was ready to sign, but Damian insisted he meet with the other attorney first. They scheduled the signing in the Houston office on Friday.

The wives joined them, and the festivities began. Food, laughter, and champagne flowed. And before long the Smith tribe joined them too. They partied beyond the closing of S&J.

Cameron occupied a chair enjoying the sights and sounds of his family as the gravity of the week loomed over him. His mind filled with black sequin and ruby red lipstick. As the captain of this ship, he'd had his rental picked up. He'd join the others on the flight back to Houston. He'd enjoy the peace of his bed soon. He let his eyes close, his head fell back against the wall.

"Cam, thank you again."

He opened his eyes and smiled at the glassy-eyed

Isaac in the seat next to him. "You're welcome. Make sure you leave tonight with the car service."

"Yes, sir." He nodded. "How'd you like tonight's show?"

Cameron wanted to bring up the subject while not encroaching on Isaac's special moment. "Man, it sealed the deal for you. The setlist flowed. It was stadium quality. I've heard you in studio sessions, but tonight I feel like I got a sample of your true sound."

Isaac smiled from ear to ear.

"Mind if I ask you a personal question?"

"Not at all."

"What's your sister's story?" He'd heard Bruce mention Sydney's stage name—Lady Bird—which meant she at least had a contract at one time. Cameron calculated the time in his mind. He had six weeks until his preliminary meeting with his cousin and the movie producers in Los Angles. They'd expect his proposed direction for the soundtrack and a few demos reflecting the sound he planned to assemble.

"That's not my story to tell."

Cameron understood, he'd use his second option. "Do you think she'll take a meeting with me?"

Isaac shrugged a shoulder. "She's kind of over the whole music industry."

Cameron didn't believe that for one second. Had he not seen Sydney on that stage he would have entertained the thought. Sydney belonged on a stage. Her voice had to be heard by the world. He sat back, considering how hard he should pursue it.

"But…"

Cameron glanced over. People saw his position as a salesman. To puff up the artist then milk them dry of their gifts. But not with RSE, they trusted him to handle the artists' gifts and desire with care. Trusted him to call the dream forward and uphold it until it manifested itself. However, the desire had to lie in their hearts. Because the dream was all, they had during the long nights of recording, the endless travel, and the constant rejection. They had to want it as much as he did or it wouldn't work.

"Her experience was different from mine."

"How so?" Cameron propped his elbow on the arm of the chair, resting his chin on his knuckles.

"I had you as a mentor. You valued my abilities, and you pushed me to explore more. I came knowing how to play the guitar, and now I play ten instruments proficiently. And now you're pushing again. I expect to work harder than I have in my life, but you've never asked me to do something that wasn't for my good. Every request has made me better. And I see tonight as another shift towards something better for myself and my future family."

"And Sydney didn't have that?"

"Not at all. You've talked a lot about legacy and the future. And as my sister, I want that for her too."

"Your instincts about her are right. You begged her because you knew she'd set the room on fire. You can't teach that. Only a few have it, and she has it in abundance. Seeing that *thing* is something you'll develop. I'm sure her being your sister helps, but as a musician and producer you want to nurture your ability to identify and mold talent."

"I guess the training starts now." Isaac chuckle.

"Nah man, your training started the moment I hired you." Cameron sat forward and gripped his shoulder. "I want to be upfront with you. I want to sign your sister to RSE. Do you think you could help make that happen?"

"Under one condition." Isaac's face turned serious. "Hear her out. Don't burn her like the last dude. That's my sister, and she's been through a lot. She just needs a second chance with people who care about her as an artist and a person."

"You got my word."

Isaac nodded.

"Bring her with you Friday." Cameron let the words hang between them.

"I can't promise anything. You see I had to beg her to come tonight."

"Oh yeah. I recall some blackmailing." Cameron laughed. "I'll sweeten the deal. We'll send the private plane, and I'll cover the shopping trip and accommodations."

"Word?" His eyebrows shot up to his hairline.

"Yes, and have your band too." Cameron wanted Sydney even if it meant coming back to Austin to have her.

"Bet." Isaac joined the others.

Cameron had six days to prepare for his meeting with Miss Sydney Jones, something told him bringing her to the Houston Headquarters would help. That woman has music in her blood, and RSE Houston was an artists' playground. He'd have all the toys and the team in place.

The energy bubbled in his stomach. He tapped his fingers on the arm of the chair trying to convince himself that her flirty words were just a song, just an act. But the images in his mind featuring his brown skin against her brown skin made him yearn to be *her* distant lover.

Cameron took a deep breath. Six days and he'd see her again. Six days to present a deal fit for a queen.

CHAPTER FOUR

"Coming!" Sydney placed the spatula aside, wiping her hands on her apron. The back to back rings told her it was Isaac. She snatched open the door. "You better be glad I love your butt."

"Good morning to you too." He kissed her offered cheek, draping an arm around her shoulder. "You are looking exceptional this morning."

Sydney stopped and turned to face him. She scanned Isaac from head to toe. His eyes looked tired. That was from partying last night, no doubt. His smile stretched to the outer edges of his face, in a Chester Cat fashion. She never liked that smile—showing all his teeth with his eyes nearly closed. It always, *always*, meant he was up to something. She turned on her heels and went back to her pancakes.

"Wait?" Isaac followed. "I didn't even say anything."

"And you don't have to." She picked up the spatula and thrust it in his direction. "The answer is no." She went back to cooking their breakfast. She'd invited him last night since she couldn't stick around. Clubs to a person prone to addictive behaviors were trouble. She only went to celebrate his twenty-fifth birthday. She glanced up from the skillet. He sat on the stool at the island, picking through her apples. "And I'm not changing my mind."

"Uh, huh." He found a piece and took a big bite.

"I mean it." His sneaky smile managed to get more wicked. "I really dislike when you do this. Why can't we be like normal people? Huh?" She walked over to the island and pulled a bowl to her side and cracked an egg on the rim. The yolk dropped in the bowl as she tossed a side glance at the clock on the stove. "But nooooo. You come, late, up to no good."

She thought she heard him laugh behind the Gala apple. They sat eyeing each other. He knew her better than anyone in the world. And she knew him. *This joker is waiting on purpose. He knows how much I love surprises.* "Tell me."

"But the answer is no." He snickered falling forward against his elbows. His face was super close to hers.

"Yes, the answer is no. Now tell me." She poured heavy cream into the bowl and lightly whisked the eggs.

Isaac laughed, and she shook her head. He managed to keep an air of youthful wonder about him. She walked back to the stove.

"I'm officially an RSE artist."

"What?" She spun around, dropping the bowl on the

island. Sydney reached for Isaac gripping his shoulders. "Congratulations!"

"Thanks, sis. I have the contract." He pulled it out.

Sydney stepped back, looking at the island where it now laid. *How had she missed it?* The drum of her heart flooded her ears as she stared at the stack of paper. Harmless really. But music contracts were her kryptonite. Debilitating, life-altering, stripping her of all her sass, her sultriness, her soul.

One misplaced signature and her entire career crumbled until all she had was a beautiful home and Isaac. No career. No fans. No music.

One Time, her ex-boyfriend and ex-manager, made sure she'd never have another record deal.

But that was her story, not Isaac's—not if she could help it. Her eyes remained locked on the contract. She realized she'd have to touch it to help. She glanced up at Isaac, and her face ached from the tight smile she tried to maintain.

"Will you look at it for me?"

The smell of smoke gave her an out, Sydney turned around and took a breath. She reached from the knob on the stove and noticed her hands shaking. She quickly turned the fire off before she burnt their breakfast and wrapped one hand inside the other.

One fool in the family was enough.

"I haven't signed." He shoved his hands in his pockets. "I won't sign it if you're not okay with it."

"Isaac, you don't mean that." This was her opportunity to support him for a change. Their roles reversed after a vital piece of her identity was ripped from her. Until last night, she thought she'd never feel that joy again. She thought she didn't want it. And now, she knew *that* was a lie. She felt like herself again.

The music flowing through her body, transforming every move into a melody. The feeling of freedom as her voice soared over the music sprinkling the audience with her essence. The inspiration of a heated gaze held too long yet not long enough.

Baby steps Bird. "What type of contract did they offer you?"

"It's a production deal."

She slowly sat at the island opposite Isaac with the contract between them. He pushed it closer to her. She suppressed a groan as his assessing eyes watched her every move. Her hand slid out, brushing her fingers against the edge of the stack. She released the pages and watched them cascade back down.

Bird it's white paper with black ink. Isaac lowered down to the stool as she scanned the words on the page.

Isaac Jones.

Rockstar Entertainment, Inc.

"Pour me a cup of coffee, please." He hopped up, and she whispered a prayer. *Knowledge is power.* "And grab a highlighter out of that drawer."

"I'll read it, but you have to get your own attorney. Don't trust theirs to look out for your best interest." The music industry was infested with blood sucking leeches. But those suckers wouldn't get their teeth in her brother. She'd given enough blood for the both of them.

"I am, and they agreed to cover the attorney's fees." Isaac sat the coffee down as her head jerked up.

"For you to use their lawyer? Low down dirty—"

"No. To use anyone I choose."

Shock coursed through her. She took a sip of the coffee and turned the page. For the next hour, she sat with him reviewing it section by section. She noticed Post Its placed near key clauses with notes scribbled in blue ink.

Review this.

Read this thoroughly.

Important.

"Who wrote these notes?" Sydney asked.

"Cameron Carter."

Sydney nodded, not knowing the name. She could see the little blue dots running down the margins as if they'd touched every inch of the agreement. She'd wished someone had done the same for her.

"I'm no expert, but this is a great deal, Isaac."

"Really?" A please smile replaced his concerned expression.

"Yes, really." She took a drink of her coffee. "It's a license deal, which means they'll have exclusive control of your masters for a limited time. They even gave a limited copyright duration."

"And that's good too?" His eyebrows shot up.

"Yes. For example, my contract isn't worth the paper they printed it on." She sat back, able to relax for the first time since he mentioned *the contract*. "Your royalty rates, should you record an album are better than fair. It's honestly unheard of. When you don't have an existing audience, music, nothing."

"They are helping me with all of that."

"How so?" Sydney sat forward, and Isaac explained the portions of the contract not written in the actual production deal. "So, basically, they are treating it like a mentorship, while giving you access to creating and producing your own music?"

Isaac nodded.

Sydney thought it sounded too good to be true. "Just make sure you get the extras in writing. You don't want them padding your expenses or expecting you to cover the costs from your royalties."

Isaac looked offended by her words.

"You asked me. And although this sounds ideal—actually *better* than ideal—you can't be too careful." She gave the contract back to him.

"I trust them. But to make you feel better, I'll have an attorney look it over."

"Great." She stood up. "Now, let me feed you."

They went about the morning reliving the night before and eating a hearty home-cooked meal. Sydney managed to create a safe haven for her self. Everything about her home reflected a new version of herself. Gone was the partying soul singer and in her place was a homebody. Although the soul singer threatened to revisit her last night.

She dropped her head as the heat flooded to her face. There was something about Mr. Suit-and-Tie that made her forget how bad that life was for her.

"Syd."

"Huh." She glanced up, she'd missed most of his story. "I'm sorry. I zoned out after they yelled surprise."

"I said, Cameron, would like to meet with you too."

"Me?"

"You wowed him."

"I can't—"

Isaac held up a hand. "RSE is not like Southern Sounds."

They were in her living room with a movie playing in the background. She glanced over his shoulder at the screen, she'd missed her favorite part. Richard Gere stood through the sunroof with a bouquet of flowers calling out to Julia Roberts. The rich man overlooking all her flaws and offering Vivian a new life. A clean slate. *Only in the movies.*

"I just can't do it again. Besides I'm still under contract, *I think.*"

"What would it hurt to hear him out?"

"And what's in it for you?" He came over here to get her opinion. He's never asked before, so why now? She dropped her feet to the floor and faced him. He looked away. "Isaac, what's in it for you? Is that why you came over here asking for my opinion? You don't need my permission to do *you.* I'm good."

"You're good?"

"I'm good." She grabbed their dirty dishes and went to the kitchen. She could feel him behind her. "So, when do you leave?" The dishwasher rattled as she placed the cups in with a little more force than she intended.

"*We* leave tomorrow." He turned her to him. "Can you please drop this attitude long enough for me to tell you about our trip?"

"*Our* trip?" She shook her head.

"He is sending a private plane, covering your shopping spree and—"

"And?"

"And, your accommodations."

She crossed her arms leaning a hip against the counter. "And this *he* is Cameron...."

"Yes, Cameron Carter." The slow smile spreading across his face made her want to poke his eyes out.

"In exchange for *what*?" Truth was she weaseled a shopping trip out of her brother, but she didn't need the extra clothes. She only planned to give him a hard time, since he was making the big bucks. But she wasn't doing too bad herself.

"A moment of your time." He closed the dishwasher and turned the dial. "And sis...you need to move on."

Sydney held up a finger to cut off the unsaid words. "Don't go there."

"Bird?"

She leaned over the island and grabbed his contract.

"We *need* to go there. You should be real tired right now."

"Tired?" She shoved it against his chest. "This visit is done."

"Are you telling me you're not the least bit curious?"

"Last night was...last night. Singing isn't an option anymore."

"And you sit back, and let him win?"

Sydney looked away.

"My sister...*my big* sister was fearless. When you see *her*, please tell her. There's a contract in Houston with her name on it." He kissed her cheek. "Goodnight Bird."

THERE'S A CONTRACT IN HOUSTON WITH MY NAME ON IT. Sydney couldn't move. That wasn't the truth. She'd cleaned the kitchen top to bottom and back up again. She scrubbed at a speck on the counter. Then she glanced at her cellphone. *Should I call him?*

Sydney tossed the towel in the sink and went to her office. She opened the drawer and pulled out her notebook and a pen, taking them back to the living room. She curled up in the couch letting the gel pen scribble across the page.

Writing was the next best thing. But her mind was blank. She balanced the pen between her fingers, tapping it against the page.

My big sister was fearless.

Sydney was fearless. *Was.*

Isaac didn't know the whole story. Her contract with Southern Sounds required one more album from her. But One Time didn't want her sober. And he wanted her in his bed again, which wasn't happening.

The only saving grace was Sydney kept her publishing contract separate from her record deal. Royalties for past records made her a wealthy woman. Writing didn't fill the same space in her heart. But One Time made sure no one would buy her new music. No one in the industry wanted to rouse the dark giant. So, she stopped trying. Stopped shopping demos to record labels. Stopped recording music.

Rejection stifled the fearless woman in her. The *fight* in her. It showed her talent wasn't enough. Heart wasn't enough. Not when music had her heart and with that came the stage, the traveling, and the rockstar vices. Sydney's sobriety needed—demanded—her to tread lightly.

Because just like music, One Time, had once been a necessity, an obsession, and look at where it landed her. But unlike people, music never failed her. No, she failed it when she wrongly thought he loved her more than her voice.

I trust them.

Could she trust RSE too? There was only one way to find out. She'd go and listen, and she'd be in Houston, should Isaac need her help. The plan seemed reasonable, but her fear of rejection wouldn't back down without a fight.

What if.... They expected Lady Bird to walk in the room with her stage hair and sparkling evening gown and her signature red lips.

What if.... They learned about her near drug overdose.

What if.... They refused to take a stand against One Time and Southern Sounds.

Sydney sat up straight. Ignorance contributed significantly to her less than graceful fall. She'd since decided she couldn't fight what she couldn't see. She couldn't fight what she didn't know.

They'd have to tell her to her face. Worse case, she'd get a free trip to Houston on a private plane. Best case, she'd witness her brother sign the contract of a lifetime. Either way, she knew one thing for sure, *Sydney took care of Sydney*. A contract couldn't make her or break her again. She'd been there and done that. She'd sit with RSE if only to hear them out.

She dialed Isaac's number. He answered on the first ring.

"I'll meet with RSE."

CHAPTER FIVE

*C*ameron cataloged the thoughts racing through his head. His Google search on Sydney "Lady Bird" Jones was…colorful. Her rise to fame and her disappearance after overdosing before a sold-out show.

Drugs.

His fingers drummed on the desk. He arrived at five o'clock after wrestling all night with how to handle today's meeting. It seemed Austin was months away and in less than a week he'd arranged a surprise for Sydney. This all happened before Google wrecked his plans.

Cameron wasn't like most music executives. He didn't follow the charts, watch YouTube videos, or sign artists because other labels wanted them. He pooled his best friends to start RSE to support his brother, and it set a precedent for the artists to come. Family first.

He scouted for artists old school. He went to dive bars, whole-in-the-wall concerts, and open mics. He let his ear do the heavy lifting. But talent wasn't enough. The artist needed a killer work ethic and outstanding integrity. RSE aspired for excellence and drugs were non-negotiable. Not even recreationally.

The music industry was brutal. The shelf life of artists ran short and mixing lousy press, and questionable character only made it worse. They could not afford to invest millions into an artist just to have them blow it up their noses.

Poor behavior led to bad press. Bad press triggered bad reviews. Bad reviews was a slippery slope to never never land. The land of one-hit wonders and obscurity.

Anything perceived as questionable character attracted the gossip hounds, and all they needed was one wayward fact to construct and destroy years of hard work.

Perception is everything.

And as if that wasn't enough, he couldn't stop thinking about her. And he'd have to once she signed with RSE. He'd replayed that night over and over in his head. He couldn't recall the last time a woman had occupied his every waking thought. Then last night she crept into his dreams.

He wanted to pretend it was merely a physical response. He'd never sugar coated things, and the truth was he wanted Sydney Jones. *Music or not.* This while knowing she could have a drug problem.

Cameron dropped his head into his hands, rubbing his tired eyes. He couldn't sleep. He couldn't think. And in less than an hour, she'd be here.

"Is she here yet?" Bruce asked breaking up the vicious cycle of his thoughts.

"Not yet. The driver called, they should arrive in about twenty minutes." He'd have to tell the guys about her past. They had a strict moral code of conduct and drugs were a dealbreaker.

"I know that look. Spill it." Bruce walked into his office.

"Close the door behind you."

Bruce sat in the chair.

Cameron glanced over at his best friend knowing he could tell Bruce anything. They became friends in the womb since their fathers were best friends. He knows all of Cameron's secrets. Yet his simmering attraction for Sydney felt off limits. Maybe it was because he knew he shouldn't want her. But he does.

"I'm not sure signing Sydney is an option for us."

"Why not?"

"What do you know about her?"

"She's an R&B pop singer. She had a few big hits, toured with a lot of major artists. Then she disappeared a few years back."

"I'm not sure she's RSE material." Cameron leaned back with a slight rock of his chair. He wasn't sure how much he wanted to share with Bruce. He wanted to talk with Sydney first. To hear her side of the events before coming to a final conclusion.

"I don't believe that for one second. You've talked about this woman nonstop for a week, and now she's not

RSE material. Hell, you talked her up so much I'd believe you have a ..." Bruce froze. "Oh, I see what this is about."

"What is it that you see Bruce?"

"*Playboy Carter* is thinking about retiring his fishing rod." The slow smile said *gotcha*. Bruce's head tossed back, and his laughter filled Cameron's office. "Wait until I tell the guys."

"Nah man ain't nothing to tell."

"There's way too many fish in the sea my brotha."

"And your impersonation of me is wack."

Bruce folded over laughing.

"What's so funny?" Damian poked his head around the door.

"Cam is feeling Lady Bird."

"Whaaaaat?!" Damian entered and sat next to Bruce. He'd watched his best friends find and marry the loves of their lives. Now they were fathers to his godchildren.

"Man, I'm done with this meeting." Cameron stood.

"Oh no, you don't. Sit and take this ribbing because you gave us the blues." Bruce had tears rolling down his face.

"I really hate you, dudes, right now." Cameron shook his head ready for them to really hit their stride. He had it coming.

"Hate on *loverboy*," Damian added, hiccuping to breathe.

Cameron struggled to fight back his own laughter. It was quite the shit show. And then he let go throwing his head back and laughed until his side ached, as they ran through his favorite lines.

"Keep your eyes on the prize," Damian stated in motivational speaker tone.

"Cam, when you gonna settled down, oh heavens no." Bruce wiggled his hands as if he were frightened. They bumped fists as they attempted to one-up each other.

"Alright Key and Peele, how about you take this little show on the road and out of my office."

A knock at the door got their attention, quieting their laughter.

"Come in," Cameron ran a hand over his moist eyes.

"They're in the conference room." The receptionist announced.

"We'll be there in a second."

"Y'all are some fools." They stood.

Cameron crossed the room to get his suit jacket. Then they walked together, gaining another partner as they neared the conference room until all six of them paused at the door. The others went inside as Cameron, Bruce, and Damian huddled in the hallway.

"We got your back either way." Bruce pat his back before strolling inside.

Damian's assessing gaze was worse than their jokes. "Here are the contracts."

Cameron took the offered documents, still undecided. "Any advice?"

"My father's number one rule in business is to look a man in his eyes and treat him fair." Damian looked towards the conference room and back at Cameron. "What would fairness require of you?"

"That I ask her about her past before making a final decision."

Damian nodded. Cameron couldn't believe Imani had managed to tame The Shark. Damian always had an edge about him. Always more seen than heard. But he'd changed since marrying Imani. Happiness made him a better man. They'd sent him to Houston to evict her, and instead, he married her. *Ain't that something.*

"Treat her fair. And let the chips fall where they may." Damian gave his shoulder a squeeze before entering the conference room.

They couldn't start the meeting without him. He glanced at the contracts in his hand. He ran a hand over his face. He could sign Isaac and pass on Sydney citing their moral clause. Or he could *let the music decide.* The thought flutter to the service and Cameron always trusted his instincts. They'd built the very ground he stood on. Except once when he let love overshadow that quiet whisper. But he wouldn't do that again. Pride wouldn't let him.

Cameron entered the conference room, and as if sensing his presence, Sydney glanced over her shoulder. Their eyes met. *I think I just found my wife.*

SYDNEY TOOK THE SEAT BESIDE ISAAC WITH THEIR BACKS TO the door. She'd met a string of handsome men as they entered the room, one-by-one. Each stopped to talk with Isaac.

The energy in the room shifted as the room fell silent.

Sydney glanced over her shoulder, and there was *Mr. Suit-and-Tie* from S&J. Isaac stood beside her.

"Cameron Carter." He extended a hand and Sydney fumbled to her feet on wobbly legs. Their hands touched, and the electricity rivaled the fireworks at the Times Square Ball Drop.

"Sydney Jones." At least that's what she hoped she said.

"You put on one helluva show at S&J." He smiled stepping closer as his thumb rubbed against the back of her hand. The smell of his cologne filled her nose, and his beautiful smile made her mouth water.

"Thank you." The faint whisper of her voice was embarrassing, but it was all she could do at the moment. He squeezed her hand before turning to Isaac.

"You ready?" He beamed at Isaac.

"Yes, sir I am."

Sydney watched as Cameron embraced her brother finding it interesting to witness. She and Isaac weren't raised in an affectionate environment. They rarely hugged or made any type of outward expressions of their feelings. So to see her brother interact with the RSE men, and their level of familiarity with him had her curious.

She sat back in the chair fully alert. Cameron strolled to the other end of the table. He was taller than she remembered. His suit looked custom fitted, expanding across his broad back. He stopped talking with each man, giving each his undivided attention.

"All of them are partners?" Sydney leaned over, whispering to Isaac.

He discreetly pointed out the six as Cameron made it to the head of the table with the other men flanking him. The six of them sat on one end. She and Isaac sat on the other. The arrangement could have felt overwhelming or even intimidating, but it didn't. She ran an assessing glaze over Isaac. He opted for a suit like the other men in the room. Her little brother was a grown man.

Sydney sat back, glad she'd decided to join him today. They flew in last night. She had an appointment at the spa this morning. This afternoon they shopped before arriving here. She squeezed his arm in support, he smiled at her over his shoulder and memories of their childhood flooded her. From the PJs to a private plane wasn't bad.

Then her eyes met Cameron's. His energy reached across the table stealing the air from her lungs. A promise lingering in the depths of his dark brown eyes.

Ready? Cameron mouthed.

Did they see it? Her eyes dashed around, and he pulled her into a vortex of him. Warm brown skin, close-cropped fade, strong jaw. But his mouth. Those lips looked pillow soft and his bedroom eyes.

Stop that. He leaned forward on his elbows smiling.

Who me? She pointed at herself, playing with the ruffles on her dress.

He gave her the sexiest nod known to *wo*man. Sydney dropped her gaze, crossing her legs beneath the table. She wore a casual hi-low blouse and skinny black jeans with ankle boots. She left her stage hair and clothes at home. They wanted to talk business with Lady Bird, but they'd have to settle for her representative, Sydney Jones.

She looked back up, and his waiting eyes spoke a million words. And Sydney nodded. She's ready.

"Lady and gentlemen, shall we?"

The meeting flowed. Isaac signed his contract with the extras added in writing. Before the ink dried, Sydney was clapping.

"Let's take a twenty-minute break." Cameron stood, and the meeting adjourned. "Miss Jones, can I speak with you for a moment?"

The room cleared leaving them alone. She pulled closer to the table directly in front of him. The polished wood stretched between them.

"I find myself in an interesting predicament."

"Your dramatic pause is everything." He laughed, and it relieved the thread of tension somersaulting through her body.

"That is not my intent. I'm usually not tongue-tied. But you're making this extremely difficult."

"So, I make you nervous?"

"*That* is what you got from my statement."

"Certainly, I mean I'm sort of fabulous." She teased appreciating the way his smile softened his features.

He leaned back. "I won't deny that. How about we keep it one hundred? Lay it all out on the table."

Sydney took a deep breath. "I know you're interested in signing me, but I'm in a new space in my life."

"And what space is that?"

"I can't sign a recording contract."

"You *can't*?" He leveled his gaze.

It was her turn to nod. She needed to dig a little

deeper into her own contract situation. Was it even valid after over five years of not recording? Was she free to enter another record deal? Did she want to?

"Why did you come here today Sydney, if you *can't* sign a recording contract?" She searched his face wishing she'd known him better. She didn't see anger or stress or disappointment. He didn't look happy either.

"I write." Sydney reached down into her bag and pulled out her notebook.

"I'm listening."

"The first song and fifth song from Friday's set were originals. And I'd love to write more music."

"Have you wrote for other artists?"

"Yes," she named a few of her biggest hits, he fell back in his seat gazing at the ceiling. "I write R&B, pop, gospel, hooks." She stopped talking, giving him time to think about her request. Last night she thought it over, and writing music would give her access to her true love without the stage.

"You'd cut the demos and work with Bruce?"

"Sure, if it's necessary."

He stood. "Walk with me Sydney."

Cameron had a short distance to walk with Sydney before they reached Bruce's studio. She said she can't sign, which didn't rule out her desire to join the team. He needed to convince her that RSE was her recording home. He crossed the room, extending a hand to help her up. His reaction to this woman was unfathomable. To claim a woman as wife material before he knew her was so beyond his comprehension that thinking it should be banned. But he couldn't help it.

"Are you going to stare at me all day?" She smiled.

"I could. Would that bother you?" He reached for her Lara Croft braid draped over her shoulder.

"No."

He smiled, her answer pleased him. Her blouse and jeans did little to conceal her curvy beauty. And the soothing tone of her voice, made him want to hear her sing again. Her gaze settled on his mouth and Cameron knew they had to rejoin the others.

"Did my offer help with your predicament?" She asked as they approached the Hall of Fame, extending an arm to stop him.

"No." It rolled out slowly. He turned to face her.

Up close in the light of the room he took his time appreciating her. He'd consider her light skin. Back in the day, they would've called her a redbone. Her sandy brown hair with blond highlights complimented her skin to perfection. And it made her hazel eyes appear near golden with their feline slant. He'd missed their unique hue the other night. And the trail of freckles on her cheeks was adorable.

"I told you what I want, now level with me." Her determination shone in her eyes.

"I want you for an upcoming movie soundtrack."

"But that's out." She crossed her arms over her full breast.

"Is it?"

"Yes."

"Why?"

"It's a private matter." She stepped back, he stepped forward.

"The way I see it, we're at a standstill. But we can help each other." The faint scent of warm honey swirling around her made Cameron want to pull her closer.

"How so?"

"I'll let you write for RSE working with us on this soundtrack."

"In exchange for what?"

"The deal must be exclusive, and you agree to reconsider signing with us in one year."

CHAPTER SIX

"We call this the Hall of Fame. It leads to the recording studios." Cameron placed a hand on her lower back guiding her down the long hall. Sydney stopped to marvel at the plaques. She heard Marques' music but didn't realize they'd sold so many albums.

"This wall is for Marques' accolades. And those belong to Bruce." He gestured to the walls.

"Is Marques your only artist?"

"No, Isaac too." He smiled.

Sydney walked over to the wall to see the shiny plaques up close. She read the plates. New Artist of the Year. Platinum status. "All from an indie label?" She glanced over her shoulder. It felt right having him beside her.

"Yes."

"We're ready for you Cam," Isaac said from the other end of the hall.

"Ready for what?" She asked Cameron.

"We arranged a jam session for you." The sound of chords called to her from further down the hall. She turned towards the sound. "I called in our best musicians. And I'm sure most of the guys are hanging around. I talked you up. Think you could give them a *taste* of Friday's show."

He stood close blocking her view with his massive chest.

"Off the record?" Sydney thought about One Time, she couldn't have a new track floating around without him finding out.

"This will be for my private collection. See it as you helping a worthy cause."

Sydney laughed. "That cause being?"

"You're saving my reputation." He toyed with her braid, his fingers searing her skin beneath her blouse.

"Is that so?"

"Can't have them thinking I've lost my touch." His smile was like staring into the bright sun. She could easily find herself dumb stupid of this man.

"We can't have that, now can we?"

"I'd be forever indebted."

"That sounds like a favor to me."

Cameron's laughter spilled over. "Oh no you don't, Isaac told me about you blackmailing him."

"Well, you are black, and a male." She returned his infectious smile. "And don't let Isaac fool you. That brother of mine knows how to milk me dry. But I'd do anything for him."

"That's what little brothers are for." He dropped her braid. "So, are you going to give them a little taste of Lady Bird or will it be a sample of Sydney Jones?"

"You'll have to wait and see." She turned on her heels following the sound of the instruments. She entered the studio. Cameron stood behind her. He pointed over her shoulder, calling out to Bruce. She passed her bag to Cameron and entered.

"Let me introduce you to the musicians."

Cameron left Sydney in the booth with the band. He now sat with Bruce behind the boards inside the control room. The speakers lined the walls and the computer monitors displaying the tracks faced them.

Bruce rolled closer. "What did she say?"

"No."

He snickered. "To Playboy Carter?"

Cameron shook his head. "I need to stop hiring my friends."

"Excuse me sir, but I'm my own boss." Bruce laughed.

"She wants to write instead." Cameron watched her talking with Isaac, her fingers danced through the air. "Turn on the sound."

Bruce pushed a button, and her voice filled the room as she played with the note arrangement. Isaac changed the chord progression, and she gave him a thumbs up. Bruce adjusted the sound by turning a few knobs on the console.

"Ready?" Cameron asked her through the headset.

She nodded walking over to the microphone, lifting the stand with the lyrics. She tossed her braid over her shoulder, pulling the headset over both ears.

He and Bruce moved in sync. Cameron dropped the lights in the booth, and the dials glowed inside the control room. He pushed back from the boards to give Bruce free reign to roll back and forth. Because he would in five…four…three…two…. The beat dropped.

"Turn it up, I want to feel it." He held his breath until his lungs screamed for release.

"Breathe bro." Marques pulled up beside him. He exhaled.

Cameron wrote the song not believing they'd find a voice to match the one in his head. "This is the title track." He whispered not wanting to miss a single alteration. She added a run hear and an adlib there, filling out the song as Isaac guided the band and Bruce supported the body of music.

Cameron stood up and went to his favorite spot. Good music made him see colors. The vibrancy in the imagery told him whether it would be a hit or not. His method wasn't one hundred percent foolproof. But it had served RSE well.

He laid on the black couch and closed his eyes. Vibrant blues and yellows turned into earth greens. The song faded out, and Marques went crazy.

"Sydney ran that song in one take!"

Cameron opened his eyes. Bruce sat on the end of the chair waiting for his response.

"That's the one." His eyes found hers, "She's the one."

SYDNEY FELL INTO BED EXHAUSTED THROWING THE COVERS over her head. They recorded all night. The focused look on Cameron's face didn't tell her much. She thought he liked it. But he spent most of the night laid back on the couch.

They sent for food. Then junk food. And he remained frozen, except for his eyes. After each take, they sought her out.

"Do you think he liked it?"

"He loved it." Isaac planned to drop her off and decided to take a quick nap on the couch.

"How do you know? He didn't say a word."

"And he won't. Cameron will mumble a word or two to Bruce. It's weird. He's like psychic or something." He punched the pillow a few times, satisfied he laid down.

"Psychic?" She tossed back the covers looking over at Isaac. "Are you pulling my leg?"

He laughed, his eyes struggling to remain open. "No, Cameron can predict a hit. I've seen him do it."

Hum. They exchanged numbers before leaving. Cameron asked her to think about his offer. Then he vanished. She'd thought he was disappointed in her recordings. It took her a few songs to get back into the groove. Sydney was rusty. That was the first time she'd recorded in a real studio in six years. And theirs was state of the art. Nothing but the good stuff.

The best microphones. The crisp sound flowing through the headphones told her they'd spared no expense. The "booth" was large enough to hold her, Isaac's band, and a Baby Grand piano comfortably.

She rolled over on her back, unable to sleep with thoughts of Cameron. He had a quiet presence. When he spoke, people moved. Not out of intimidation but…she search her mind recalling the way he talked with the other men, the musicians, her. It was out of respect.

They played around with four songs tonight. Sydney hummed the melody of the first song, *Damaged*. But something was missing. The lyrics held an unsaid ache.

Can you pick up the pieces?
I've been shattered, I've been bruised,
I've been batter, I've been misused.
I'm damaged.
Damaged by you.

She played around with rearranging the words, wondering if they needed to add something to the melody. An hour later her brain couldn't take it, she needed sleep. She reached over and turned off the light.

Her eyes closed and a chime came from her phone. She slapped her hand around the nightstand until she found it. *Cameron Carter*, it was him.

She unlocked her phone and read the message:
Have dinner with me tonight.
Sure.

CAMERON LAID AWAKE WITH *DAMAGED* PLAYING ON REPEAT. He struggled to reconcile his attraction to her and while knowing she had a questionable past. Getting her to agree to work with RSE for a year would give them time to see her in action. To see if she was the same woman. To see if she was the woman they needed. *He needed.*

But signing her would mean he'd have to keep his hands to himself. His father and fellow group members constructed five cardinal rules of living the life of a successful artist. The *Sin*Sation rules, named after their group. And number five came to mind: Don't bed where you make your bread.

How would he be able to keep his distance?

Bedding Sydney would be pure delight. And not only for her sinful body and a wicked smile, but there was the way her eyes sparkled while inquisitive, her quick wit, bubbly laugh, and the ache in her voice conveying a million emotions with ease. Emotions he heard loud and clear.

She mesmerized the band and the crew, and she was clueless. She had no idea how good she was. She couldn't, or she'd record an album right now. And somehow she managed to have an air of innocence too.

Cameron grew up in the music industry. To say he was jaded was an understatement. People sought him out for his namesake only. His name was his brand. His access. His leash. Until he started RSE. He forged a wall protecting them from the users and opportunists while reflecting a relatable image as a brand.

Don't trust woman enthralled by the glitz and glamour of entertainment, rule number four, was his downfall in the past. His ex-Gabrielle appeared wholesome and the perfect catch until Cameron found himself entangled in a ruthless scheme. It made him a little less trusting, less willing to give his heart again. He didn't get that feeling from Sydney.

However, he'd been wrong before. *So what was he saying?*

Cameron took several deep breaths curbing the cynic in him. The part of him waiting for people to reveal their true colors. *Time reveals all things.* He'd work closely with her ensuring Sydney Jones would mesh with RSE.

Now to convince her to sign the exclusive writing deal. She had to see what he sees in her. She's a powerhouse waiting to be properly introduced to the world. And something told him it wouldn't take much to convince her. Then they'd both benefit. He'd have the counterpart to Marques for RSE, and she'd have a hit album.

Win. Win.

Now, he'd have to get to know her and somehow manage to keep his hands *and heart* to himself.

CHAPTER SEVEN

*C*ameron guided them into a private dining room. The scent of cumin and jalapeños made her mouth water as he pulled out her chair to the tune of mariachi music.

Sydney scanned the menu aware of his eyes on her. The power of his energy made it hard for her to focus, as the words blurred before her. She closed the menu thankful for the privacy of the room. She'd slept in most of the day and spent sometime around the rooftop pool. Now, she was ready to negotiate a contract with RSE.

Cameron had the power to give her back something she wanted more than her next breath, music. But holding his intense gaze, she wondered if it was possible to have him too. The thought froze in her brain settling into the space left void by her disappointing relationships in the past. Men wanted Lady Bird, they tolerated Sydney. Would Cameron be the same? Another somebody she'd have to get over?

"So, to what or whom do I owe this honor?" She said in a silky voice, using a finger to trace the rim of her glass, channeling Lady Bird.

"It's all about you. Your performance last night had the men excited about the future. So, you can thank yourself." He relaxed in the chair, poker face intact. It was his eyes that gave him away, caressing her from afar. "Would you like to order Sangria or a margarita?"

"No, thank you, I don't drink," her voice broke.

Sydney saw the ghost of something running behind his gaze, as if he were leading them somewhere. He asked about her accommodations and the shopping trip. All had exceeded her expectations.

The waiter returned and took their orders. Cameron's eyes locked with hers as if he were reading her soul. It made her feel exposed and aroused. She couldn't take it anymore.

"Is tonight business or pleasure Mr. Carter?"

"Both." Her heart hiccuped. His voice had an air of certainty. But nothing about his intensity said "business."

Sydney inhaled attempting to gain her composure, "Do you plan to dance around this obvious chemistry we have?"

"I'm not the dancing type."

"What type are you?"

"I'm in transition."

"*Transition*? What does that mean?" She held up a hand stopping his response. "And please do me a favor and be honest. I'm too old for games. I'm a big girl, you won't hurt any feelings over here." She took a drink of water.

"I don't have to lie to get a woman, Sydney. Ask me, and I'll tell you, straight up. And I'm not dancing around our attraction, I'm just having a hard time deciding what I *plan* to do about it."

The waiter returned with their food, and she remained mute. They talked about the weather, Houston traffic, and the Austin music scene as his statement hung between them.

"Mixing business and pleasure is bad business."

"We could always pass on the business." His face fell the slightest bit.

"That's not an option."

"Why?" He was disturbing in every way.

"Because I need you." His voice was low and smooth. The haze reflected in his eyes made her squeeze her thighs tighter. A woman could lose herself with a man like him.

"Me or my voice?"

"Both."

Cameron's honesty stung. She wanted him to want her, and only her. She'd traveled the whole "dating her manager" road. Cameron had it right, the two were a recipe for disaster. One Time made millions off her, and when he was finished with her, he left taking her career with him. And it left her unable to give herself completely to any man.

But something about Cameron struck her as different, starting with Isaac's reaction to him. The way people gravitated to him like trained moths to a flame. Knowledge is power, fluttered to mind. Maybe learning more about him could help her.

"Why?"

Cameron sat forward. "Why what?"

"Why me? Why now?" She left the other questions unsaid.

Why do I feel drawn to you?

Why do you make me want the very things I shouldn't? Like intimacy and companionship. *Love.*

"I think your voice is a gift the world should experience. And now because RSE has the opportunity to score our first motion picture. I want your voice on that soundtrack. But Sydney, I need *you* to keep it one hundred with *me*." He turned her words on their head. "I'm willing to offer you the writing contract, if you'll work with Bruce."

"And…." His pregnant pause called up her fears and uncertainties. "We have a strict moral code of conduct for our entire team. No drugs or excessive drinking." His hands emphasized the words.

"I haven't used drugs or had a drop of alcohol in five years. And I don't plan to start."

"Are you sure?" He stared back in waiting silence. *Was he baiting her?*

"Cameron say what you need to say." An edge of dread creep up her spine, panic rioted in her. Would she always be remembered for that one night? Hundreds of shows. Millions of records sold. Yet, Sydney had to find a way to overshadow her youthful ignorance. To move on. To be seen once again for her talent, not her mistakes.

"I want you but not at the cost of what we're building. This is a huge opportunity for all of us, and I can't gamble on you and lose."

"I'm not going to ruin my second chance. This is a gamble for me too." Her voice cracked.

Cameron dropped his head as if in thought. She waited pushing the food around her plate. She wasn't foolish. She knew people didn't get second chances often and she was tired of living closed up in her house hiding from the world. Hiding from Lady Bird's arrogance and naiveté. Trusting the wrong people led her down the yellow-brick road and straight to hell. And she was still trying to crawl her way back.

She'd forgiven herself, and now it was time to move on, her brother had yet to steer her wrong in the past. And something told her she'd do well gambling on RSE. And Cameron.

"Music is it for me, Cameron. I'd live, eat, drink it if I could. And I want it back." His eyes held hers. "Give me a contract, and I'll work with Bruce night and day to make this soundtrack happen."

"Will you reconsider singing on at least *Damaged*?" She broke eye contact with him as mixed feeling surged through her. Dread. Excitement. Hope. "Please."

Sydney had a feeling Cameron didn't say *please* often. He didn't come across as rude or demanding, but the soft plea beneath the word made her relent, a little. She nodded not sure what it would mean and if it would bring One Time out of hiding.

A look of relief washed over his face. Then Cameron stuck out his hand, "Welcome to RSE."

SYDNEY TOOK HIS OUTREACHED HAND. HER MUCH SMALLER hand cradled inside his and a current sparked between them. "Thank you," she whispered.

"I hope you're ready. Bruce may have you second-guessing your decision." He tried to ease the sexual tension, but it proved impossible. He'd spent most of the day debating his growing feelings for her. It was unlike any he'd felt before, not even with Gabrielle.

"Well, you better have them draft the contract quick." She laughed.

They resumed eating with the contract out of the way. They both seemed to relax and enjoy dinner.

"Would you like dessert?"

She shook her head her curls bounced with each movement. "I can't. You'll have me rolling into the booth if I eat another bite."

"Okay, suit yourself. I'd like a slice of tres leches cake." Cameron paused waiting for the waiter to leave before shifting their conversation. He wanted to know more about the woman unknowingly challenging every rule and boundary he'd established for himself. "Tell me something I won't find on the internet."

"Let's see." She wiped her mouth with the napkin. "I lived in my car for almost two years."

"When?"

Her faint smile held a touch of sadness. "You want the

short or long version."

"Long."

"I moved from Kansas City to LA with less than two hundred dollars to my name. I had no contacts and no job."

"How old were you?"

"Twenty-one. Youth makes you feel invincible." She shook her head at the memory. "I barely graduated high school because I spent my nights singing at any club willing to give me a shot. Then I slept through all my classes."

"My parents would have killed me."

"We were raising ourselves. I'd do it differently if I could. But I always knew I wanted to sing. I felt school had nothing to offer me. It was a waste of time in my book. So I made my rounds to all the clubs and talent shows until one night a manager," she air quoted, "convinced me that L.A. was where I needed to be."

"I take it he wasn't a manager."

"No, he was a weasel in a cheap suit." Her nose wrinkled in disgust, Cameron laughed. "But his words planted a seed in me. I knew I had no chance of getting a deal if I stayed in Kansas City. So I packed my bags, gassed up my old Toyota Corolla, and drove to California."

"Fearless."

"Ignorant." Her expression was tight with strain. "I got there, and the weasel was a sewer rat. He couldn't keep his hands to himself, and I couldn't go back."

"Did you ever hear from the weasel again?" He

couldn't imagine. He reached out lacing his fingers with hers. He'd always had his family or his friends.

"No. I had to stretch the little money I had. I found a job as a waitress at a dive bar that let me sing for tips. I used a gym membership to shower. And I slept in my car until I saved enough to rent an apartment with a co-worker."

The waiter brought the cake, and Cameron forked the moist milk cake. "Have you ever tried it?"

"No, I'm not much of a sweets person, unless it's pancake syrup."

"I'll have to remember that." He liked her animated facial expressions. "Here, try it." He wanted to scrub her mind clear of the memory, to see her smile. He extended the fork in her direction with his eyes trained on her lips. She had that red lipstick on again and like before it caused his brain to run wild with inappropriate thoughts.

Sydney leaned forward taking the cake, her throaty groan made heat curse through his body.

"That tastes like heaven covered in whipped cream."

Cameron noticed a dollop of cream on the side of her mouth. He wrapped her napkin around his finger, slowly rubbed it away.

"No more cake for you." He teased trying to calm his racing heart.

"That's too bad, I was just about to ask for another bite." His eyes found hers, and they shone like gold. He dropped the fork as the temperature in the room increased by several degrees.

"Baby you're playing with the wrong one." His gruff

response slipped out, but he meant it. He had to invoke every life and business skill known to man to keep her at a distance. But sampling her was much more appealing, and the sensual way she just darted her tongue across her lips, had him fighting a losing battle. Because he wanted Sydney Jones.

"I'm starting to think you're exactly the one." A mischievous look covered her beautiful face.

Cameron, the master negotiator, was at a loss for words. *Change the subject or take her home.* Those were the only two choices he could pluck from his scrambled thoughts. He snapped his eyes closed as a vision of her sprawled across his bed came to mind. But losing control wasn't an option. His attempt to focus on the music with sultry Sydney near proved impossible.

"Are you going to behave Miss Jones?" His rising manhood could careless that she was an RSE artist.

"Only if you make me," she stared with longing at him. "Which brings to mind an idea."

"I'm listening."

"I'm interested in getting to know you better." She leaned forward and used his fork to pick up a morsel of cake. "Or will that violate your *strict* moral code of conduct?"

Cameron's mouth watered for the sweetness headed his way. Then it hit him, like a sucker punch from Tyson, "You're trying to seduce me, Miss Jones."

"Yes, Mr. Carter I am. That way you don't have to decide what to do about our head-spinning attraction."

She sat back with a pleased look on her face as the

sweet cake melted on his tongue.

"What exactly are *we* negotiating here?" Her boldness piqued his curiosity as he considered the options. Because if his body had its way he'd break all five of the *Sin*Sation rules tonight!

"I'd like to get to know you."

"And I'd like the same." His response pleased her judging by the high voltage smile. "After hours."

"Yes, sir." she saluted.

He crooked his finger beckoning her forward. Sydney stood up smoothing her dress before walking the short distance.

HE STEPPED FORWARD SLIPPING SYDNEY'S ARMS AROUND HIS neck. Then his hands lazily contoured her waist, hips, and settled on her bottom.

"I think we should seal this deal with a kiss," Cameron whispered his hot breath against her ear.

His lips captured hers, and Sydney sagged into his strong arms. He moved his mouth over hers, she slipped him a little tongue. His lips warm, coaxing, and demanding as shivers of delight followed his exploring hands. He broke the kiss, but Sydney needed one more taste.

She gripped his neck and pulled him down for a repeat, and he didn't disappoint. He adored her mouth with his tongue, setting fire to her soul. She pulled back.

Panting. Breathless. Aching.

Bird, what have you done?

CHAPTER EIGHT

*S*ydney and RSE finalized her contract and tonight she'd have her first session with Bruce. Truth be told, she was nervous. Isaac came by the hotel to "help" by telling her what to expect, but that only made it worse.

She entered the building waiving at security. "Cam wants to see you before you head back."

"Okay, thanks." She glanced at her watch and turned towards his office. She tugged at her oversized t-shirt wishing she'd worn something nicer. They'd talked over the phone daily. But tonight was the first time they'd see each other since dinner a few nights ago. She knocked lightly on his door.

"Come in." He motioned to the chair. She sat as he finished the phone call. This man works around the clock. Who takes business calls at 11:30? She noticed a wall of pictures and stood to get a better look.

She recognized a few faces. He ended the call and

came up behind her wrapping his arms around her waist. She leaned back.

"Is this your family?"

"Yes." He kissed the side of her neck. "Those are my parents Michelle and Curtis Carter. You know Marques. That's Kyle and my baby sister Lauren."

"Your sister?" All of their faces reflected the same smile in various hues of warm brown except Lauren. Her ivory skin was a direct contrast to the others.

"Yes, she's adopted."

"Oh, you all look happy."

"Mom made us." He laughed. They looked like a perfect family dressed in white shirts and denim bottoms. His parents stood in the middle beaming with pride. "That's an old picture. Here's the most recent one."

He walked her over a few steps. They had the same smiling faces with a couple additions.

"That is Brione, Marques' wife, and my angel Kayla and baby AJ."

She glanced at him over her shoulder. "You have a beautiful family."

"Thank you. This is my current favorite." He tapped the frame a few pictures over. "This is our RSE family. Bruce and his wife, Sandi with their three kids. Damian and his wife Imani with their son. Marques and his family. And you've met the rest of the guys and Eliana. Isaac is somewhere in there too."

"When was that picture taken?" They all wore matching RSE t-shirts.

"Last year and we're growing. You'll meet everyone at

our annual picnic. It makes taking the picture easy." He grabbed her hand and walked back to the chairs in front of his desk. She glanced at his wall of memories once more.

"Nervous?"

"Yes! And Isaac's pep talk fell flat. I don't know what to expect."

Cameron laughed, "Just do what Bruce says, and it will be a breeze."

"Are you lying to my face, Mr. Carter.?"

His head fell back, "A little. To be the best you have to work with the best. Bruce is the best."

She nodded. Southern Sounds didn't have a grooming process. "Do you plan to develop all of your artists?"

He sat back with their hands intertwined. "No doubt. I took a page out of Motown's book. Plus that's how my father prepared us."

"That's right, he's in a music group."

"Yep, the SinSations. And they're still going strong with all the original members except one. He passed about twelve years ago."

"I'm sorry to hear that."

"Thanks." He stood pulling her to her feet. "We wanted to develop our artists in-house. Artistry first, then profit."

"That sounds too good to be true."

"How so?"

"Most record labels are all about the streams and album sales. If you don't have a Top 10 record out the gate, you get bumped."

"I guess that is the norm." They stepped into the hall-way, and he dropped her hand. She missed the warmth. "We are fortunate that we have other business ventures, together and apart. We make wise financial choices, thanks to Jamal, but we're not pressed to turn a profit. Fortunately, that hasn't been an issue." They stopped at the studio door. "I'll let you go inside. I'll come back to check on you later."

He kissed her cheek and rounded the corner back to his office. Sydney glanced up to make sure the light was off and opened the door.

Bruce was sitting behind the control board. He seemed to live in that chair.

"Hey Sydney, you ready to get to work?"

"Yes."

"Have a seat?" He pointed to the couch.

She nodded dropping her bag and sat down. They'd talked a couple times, mostly pleasantries. He seemed to balance out the rest of the guys. He had a relaxed vibe. He rarely talked, and he always had a smile on his face.

"How are you? Bruce sat forward looking at her intently.

"Nervous." She smiled.

"Don't be. That's why I want to talk first." She nodded, pulling out her notebook and a pen. "We have roughly four weeks to pull together a sound for the soundtrack. Which means you and I will have to pull double sessions most days to get a feel for each other."

"What do you mean?" She leaned forward.

"I need to get to know your vibe. And you'll learn

mine. I will make suggestions to make our efforts gel but expect to have a few bumps in the road." He paused for a moment. "Cameron will oversee our progress. And as stated in the contract, he has the final word on everything that leaves this studio."

"Will we work on songs I have or write new material?"

"I hope both. This first week I'll split our efforts. We'll use one session to play with your sound and the second session towards the soundtrack."

"Will we work with other artists?"

"Yes." He nodded. "I don't expect you to attend all the soundtrack sessions. But your scheduled sessions are mandatory. We want to include RSE artists on the sound-track. Plus the movie has a few singers in the cast. They'll fly out in a couple of weeks. We'll need to have fresh material for them to test."

"Wow!"

"Tell me about IT. This is a lot to throw at you, but Cameron believes you can do it."

"And what about you?"

"I'll let you know after a few sessions. I know you've recorded before, but working with other artists is not the same as knowing your own voice. The more we work together, the more we'll feel each other out."

"I understand. Is there anything you need from me?"

"Be on time. Communication is vital with such a tight timeline. Most of my artists I've developed for years. So, let's agree to extend grace to each other as we find our way towards the goal." She returned his smile. "Any questions?"

"No, not that I can think of."

"Cool. Expect to run from midnight to seven. We usually order food and break around three or so. It's not set in stone, but it gives a basic timeline."

"Sounds good. I guess it's time to get to work."

"You got it. For tonight I've pulled a few of your previous songs. We'll play around with them. I want us to work on remixes. The goal is to identify your sound. We'll start with *Ashes*."

Sydney balance on the end of the couch. This was like a boot camp. She'd gone from working in her garden in Austin to working in a music studio.

"Grab a chair sit over here at the board. Did you write this song?"

"Yes. Years ago. But it's one of my favorites." She followed his instructions, sitting next to him.

"Good…good." He clicked around on the board, and the song played through the speakers. "Is this the sound you want to develop? A soulful-pop sound."

"Yes and no. I want to keep the soul but drop the pop." She smiled as he bobbed his head to the song. "For example, originally I wrote the hook to go like this."

Sydney leaned forward so Bruce could hear her over the music, singing the original melody. Southern Sounds rejected it, stating it wouldn't crossover.

"I like that." He paused the music. She eyed the keyboard across the room. "Do you play?"

"Yes."

"Word?" A twinkle danced in his eyes. "Let me see what you can do."

Sᴍᴅɴᴇʏ ꜰᴇʟᴛ ʟɪᴋᴇ ᴀ ᴋɪᴅ. Sʜᴇ ᴀɴᴅ Bʀᴜᴄᴇ ʙᴏᴜɴᴄᴇᴅ ᴀʀᴏᴜɴᴅ the studio from instrument to instrument. She rewrote the bridge, and he revamped the beat.

"Now for the fun part," Bruce whispered. He clicked around on a computer then rolled in his chair back to the board. "It's time to jump in the booth."

She stood up with the lyrics in hand.

"I know you know the words. But I need you to follow my led. When you get to this part," he mumbled the words leading to the bridge, "try it like this." Bruce sang the words and her mouth hit the floor.

"You sound amazing."

"No, ma'am. I can hold a note on a good day for the others, I'm a poor substitute compared to *real* singers like you." He chuckled. "Go inside and grab the headset. Keep your eyes on me for this first cut."

Back in the booth. She went inside and grabbed the headset, settling it over her ears. Bruce threw up a thumb for the sound level. She used her finger to point up to increase the sound until it was just right. Throwing up an "okay" sign she placed the lyrics on the stand.

She wrote *Ashes* before life caught up to her. The words took on a new meaning. Ashes remained after the original matter burned, no longer what it was. Something new, void of color, now a remnant.

The analogy mirrored her life and career. She could

point the finger at her management, her label, the doctors giving out pills like candy. But the second step to her recovery had been taking responsibility for her action. Her first step was deciding to choose her life over everything.

Money, fame, and her contract be damned.

Sydney gambled with the devil and lost. And her once precious career burnt to a crisp. A fleeting depiction of something that meant so much. And standing in the RSE booth, she felt Bruce's excitement, Isaac's encouragement, and….

"Do it again," Bruce said.

She opened her eyes and saw Cameron standing over Bruce's shoulder. She felt his determination. Yes, for RSE to make the project a success but for her too. He thought enough of her voice to take a chance *on her*.

"Sydney sing this song and mean it. Each word should have a face or memory attached. Don't have a memory use one from a movie. Find your inspiration and hold on to it. Everything is gone, and now you have a chance to start over. This run is not about perfection. Make me a believer. " Bruce rolled in his chair sliding left and right. Her focus was locked on Cameron. "Run it again."

Cameron moved to a dial and lowered the lights. From the booth, all she saw were the board lights reflecting off his face. Then he was gone. He went to his favorite spot on the couch. Armed with her inspiration she gave the song a new meaning in her heart. Instead of focusing on what she lost, she would sing about what she gained.

This one's for Cameron.

Bruce added strings to the opening notes with only her voice. Eyes closed she dug deep, visualizing the fires in her life. Her parents. Her career. Her confidence. It was time to emerge from the ashes a new woman.

CAMERON HEARD THE SHIFT IN HER VOICE. THE VULNERABLE ache when her voice cracked. The sheer power behind her steeled them.

She stood like a strong statue, eyes closed, reaching into space when the music built, expanding to a robust instrument arrangement. Then it pulled back for her final line word, barely audible.

"…baby I'm blowing in the wind…"

The emotional declaration seeped into his pores.

"You gotta get her to stay," Bruce whispered.

"I know."

CHAPTER NINE

*C*ameron was scheduled to leave for LA on Tuesday. He entered RSE, eyes trained towards the executive suite. Damian handled building the Houston Headquarters. Their five-acre compound gave them plenty of space for the studios and large executive offices. Most days he loved his office, but it was rare that they called him in for an "issue." He dropped his briefcase in his office and went directly to Bruce's studio.

He crossed the doorway, and the energy hit him. Sydney sat arm crossed on the couch, her leg bouncing as if thoroughly agitated. Bruce sat in his high back chair with his back to the booth. The two hit a rough patch, so rough Cameron was called in to mediate.

His best friend and the woman he was growing quite fond of regarding each other as enemies. Bruce tossed a quick wink before his face went back blank. *This is part of his process.* Cameron rolled his eyes. He'd have to play the bad guy.

"What's the problem?" He lowered into the free chair, keeping his gaze on her.

"Ladies first," Bruce mumbled.

"How kind of you?" Her expression was a mask of stone. "Run it again. Run it again. Run it again. How many times do we have to run the damn thing before its done?" She took to examining her unpolished nails.

Cameron turned his face to the ceiling calling on the Man above for help with his lady. *His lady*...the thought lodged in his head. He saw Sydney as his, and it scared the hell out of him. They'd only known each other a month. But spending time with her here and there established a rhythm between them, and he wanted more.

He looked over at Bruce and mouthed, *You owe me big time*. He rolled closer to her on the couch.

"Sydney, baby," his voice dropped in volume, "this is part of the process. You told me you'd 'live, eat, drink it if I could,' now is the time."

"Cameron don't baby me. I'm not singing that song again. 'Change that word.' 'Sing that line.' *'Run it again!'*" She mocked Bruce and man was she mad. "And if he says 'Run it again' one more time I swear I'm gonna scream, Cameron. And I mean it. *Scream*."

"Sydney I'm sorry, but this is Bruce's call."

"I'm...not...singing it again." The word stretched out in a lethal tone, her neck rolling let him know she meant business, but so did he.

"Your Royal Highness, we don't sit on our butts. You do as the producer says or you're locked out of the studio."

"Locked out!" She popped to her feet, her eyes blazing golden fire.

"I didn't stutter." Cameron knew exactly what was going on. "Sydney you can't expect to get better if you don't want to be challenged. You both have a job here. I do too, and it's not serving as a referee. I have a class to teach at the center. Get your bag. You're going with me."

He could kill Bruce for putting him in the middle. Cameron trusted him but having a standoff with Sydney was not his idea of a good time. She looked like she wanted to charge him.

Cameron grabbed his briefcase and waited at the front door for Sydney. "Chop, chop, the kids are expecting me."

Sydney picked up her pace. He examined her face and noticed the bags under her eyes. He'd take her to Harmony Dance then back to the hotel to rest. He pushed the glass door open, and she dragged her feet to the car.

Sydney got in the car with a huff. He sat behind the wheel, turning to look at her directly.

"Baby, when is the last time you slept more than a few hours?"

"I'm not talking to you Cameron Carter, no matter how many times you call me baby." She gave him a sideways glance.

"What if I said, *please baby baby baby please*?"

She was fighting the urge to laugh, she shook her head. He started making loud kissing noises, and she burst into a full-hearted laugh.

"Now kiss me, woman."

"Only because you said please." She pulled him close and kissed him slowly. "I needed that."

"Buckle up. We are heading to Harmony Dance. It is owned and operated by Damian and his wife, Imani." They made it in record time. Cameron hopped out and rounded the car to her door. "We all volunteer in different capacities. Today I'm teaching a music business class."

They entered and the building, it was crowded as usual for a Saturday morning. He guided Sydney down the hall. "You can join me or hang out with Imani. Let me see if she's in her office," he peaked. "Hey, beautiful!"

"Save your flirting for some poor unsuspecting woman." She laughed, and he shook his head. "I have company."

"I'm sorry." She stepped out.

"Imani Hughes I'd like to introduce you to—"

"Lady Bird, it is great to meet you."

"Thank you, and please call me Sydney."

Cameron should have known that Imani would know Sydney. "Imani spent time traveling as a professional dancer until returning to Houston to open Harmony Dance."

"Don't leave out the best part," Imani chimed in, "They sent Damian to evict me." She placed a hand on her hip.

"We did, but she is making it sound much worse than it really was." He answered the question look on Sydney's face. "How are you feeling?"

"I'm tired of being pregnant." She laughed. "Go to

your class. Sydney can hang with me. The ladies should be here shortly for brunch."

"The ladies?"

"Yes, it's first Saturday." Imani smiled, and Cameron wondered if he could cancel his class.

"Sydney, come with me." He reached for her hand.

"Oh no, you don't." Imani pushed him toward the classroom.

He turned for a final attempt. "Sydney believe only half of what you hear."

Their laughter followed him down the hall. He knew Sydney would have a great time, but he was slightly concerned about what they'd tell her. *Please, Lord, don't let them mention Playboy Carter.*

He entered the classroom with a plan in mind for the evening. Sydney being locked out was the perfect opportunity to spend some time together. They'd squeezed in a few minutes, here and there. But sticking to his *after-hours* requirement made it hard. He'd found himself wanting to hang out in the studio all day just to be near her. But he had a label to run and a class to teach.

SYDNEY SPENT THE MORNING WITH THE WIVES OF RSE. *Who are these people?* They had an air of *this is too good to be true* about the entire morning.

A catered brunch and it only took thirty minutes to relax. They joked and teased about everything from their husbands to their kids. And they about died when she told them Bruce got her locked out this morning.

"What did you do?" Sandi, his wife, asked.

"I told Cameron if he said 'Run it again' one more time that I'd scream."

They laughed so hard Sydney thought Imani would have the baby. She held her belly and rocked back and forth as tears rolled down her face.

"Are you all in the industry too?" Sydney asked enjoying their company.

"Not really." Brione, Marques' wife, answer. "I'm an ex-lawyer, but now I work as a co-manager for my husband with Cameron."

"As you already know, I run Harmony Dance. I was a professional dancer, now I handle the dancers and any choreography." Imani added.

"Bruce and I have a cafe, Coffee Confessions. You should stop by sometime, although I don't work much now that we have the kids. I mostly take care of my family and help out around Harmony." Sandi said bouncing a little one on her knee.

Sydney had one sibling, Isaac, and never had many girlfriends. She could get used to hanging out with these women. They knew how to have a good time. Plenty of food and laughs to spare. They ate then cleaned up while discussing details for the annual RSE picnic.

"So Brione you're a lawyer?" Sydney asked wiping down a table. She'd been giving her contract with Southern Sounds a lot of thought. After working with

Bruce on the soundtrack, she wanted her voice to stay on a few of the songs.

"I was." Brione stopped and picked up the crying AJ —Andrew, Jr.

Sydney pinched his chubby cheeks and brushed away his tears.

"Do you need some help with something?" Brione asked.

Sydney glanced at the other ladies, she felt comfortable with sharing. "I'm not sure if my old music contract is still valid. I'd love to have someone look at it."

"Have you told Cameron? Brione asked.

"No, I kind of want to handle it myself." They nodded.

"Here's my husband's card," Imani said. "If there's something to be found, Damian will find it."

"And that includes every grimy little detail. He helped me out a few years ago. He's a saint." Brione said.

"And The Shark." Imani teased.

Sydney took the card. "Thank you."

"Babe, you ready?" Cameron called out as he entered the room. All eyes were on her.

"Somebody is holding out on us," Imani said in an awfully loud whisper.

"Now I see why my husband kicked her out." Sandi teased. They bunch laughed them right out the center.

Back in the car, Cameron glanced over at her, "You have a choice, my place or yours."

"I'm too exhausted to decide."

"Mine it is." He turned the ignition over, "Let's stop and pack a bag."

SYDNEY WAS OUT BEFORE THEY LEFT THE PARKING LOT. HE glanced over at his sleeping beauty. She'd survived brunch with the RSE wives. He called Bruce after his class and found out the ordeal this morning. She'd been staying all night and the majority of the day. Bruce had pushed every button until she pushed back.

Bruce and Sydney needed a break from each other.

Cameron shook his head. He sent a group text to the guys. He was taking a few days off. They needed to get clothes and toiletries, but she slept so soundly. He made an executive decision, next stop the RSE beach house. He would have to just buy whatever they needed to last a few days once they got to Galveston.

Cameron popped in the soundtrack demo and settled in for a nice ride with his lady at his side.

CHAPTER TEN

*S*ydney opened her eyes and sat straight up alarmed. *Where am I?*

She didn't recognize the room. The sound of crashing waves caught her attention. She walked over to the window and remember she'd been in the car with Cameron. He'd said something about time off, the beach, she mumbled her agreement and went back to sleep.

"Cam." She called out, her voice echoed back.

She walked to the door and glanced into a spacious living room. There he was, sleep on the couch with his feet propped on the coffee table. His jacket tossed beside him, his tie hanging loosely around his neck, with a laptop on his lap. She leaned against the wall openly assessing him.

He surprised her.

While recording he'd pop in and out. He made sure she had meals and made it back and forth to the studio with ease. He said little, but his actions spoke volumes. So much so, that she wondered if she was out of her league.

Cameron did not compare to the men she usually dated. She liked her men with an edge—*street cred*. But they all managed to do her wrong, cheat on her, steal from her. Take while giving very little in return. They made it easy to place a "Sorry I'm Closed" sign over her heart.

She wasn't expecting Mr. Suit-and-Tie to be so attentive. Sexy? *Absolutely*. But doting and observant. Demanding yet catering.

She couldn't say he lacked an edge, it was there hidden in his dark eyes. The tailored suits, clean haircut, made him appear perfect. *Always* ready. *Always* put together. The tamed heat in his eyes, let her know it lingered beneath the service.

Sydney watched him and the RSE tribe, as they called it, for the past month. They were like the Huxtables to her PJs. The Brady Bunch to her Married With Children. And Isaac fit right in with them. They made no difference between him and the others. Priding themselves on "family."

A word she'd never quite experienced either.

They were rich—scratch that, wealthy. Second and third generation wealthy. Their kids, kids, *kids* would be wealthy. *Who sends a private plane for a meeting?* Funding million dollar charity organizations. Buying out exotic islands. Scoring a major motion picture soundtrack because your cousin asked.

Wealthy people.

But what punctured a ginormous hole in her thinking was their generosity. Their kindness exceeded anything she'd ever expected from people like them. And she was wrong because they were a real family, and something she'd never had. It was just her and Isaac.

A vision of the RSE wives sitting around at brunch laughing and passing around their babies. What she wouldn't give to have that?

Sydney slowly removed his laptop and placed it aside. Then she sat on the floor. She went after him for a good time. Instead, she'd found herself in new territory.

Lady Bird would jump his bones, let him wine and dine her, and move on. But Sydney was tired of being alone. Tired of always having her own back.

Lady Bird would find a way to sabotage it before Cameron had a chance to walk away. Sydney knew she could have it all. But she had to leave fear behind no matter how much she distrusted people in the music industry.

She had to find fearless Sydney.

Give it a shot, a voice inside insisted. And then what?

She drew her knees to her chest bracing herself from the unknown. But unlike men in the past, a relationship with Cameron wouldn't mean settling. That was if she didn't count his "after hours" request. Which made sense, right?

The CEO and the employee.

The music executive and the artist.

Maybe he was right, it made for bad business.

But did bad business feel like this? He made her smile with his antics like the annoying kissing noises. The way he called her baby today.

Baby....

Cameron shifted on the couch, crossing his arms over his chest. *Knowledge is power.* Knowing was better than not knowing. Just like her record deal. She planned to reach out to Damian next week. No more hiding. No more waiting for One Time to destroy her life. She'd survived once, she'd do it again.

Cameron said something about hanging out for a few days. She'd use this time to see if they could have more than stolen moments. If not, she'd enjoy the time they have together, and when they wrap the soundtrack, she'd head back to Austin with no regrets.

Sydney felt the cool breeze coming from the patio door. She stood and quietly moved to the chair, grabbing the fuzzy blanket. She draped it over Cameron and placed a soft kiss on his forehead. She turned off the light and went back to the bedroom.

Sydney found a fluffy white bathrobe and decided to take a long bubble bath. She emerged an hour later a new woman.

She now went in search of her phone to call Isaac. They'd left for a few shows in Chicago earlier in the week. She looked around the bedroom and didn't find it.

Cameron must have it, she thought. She went back to the living room.

"Hey, gorgeous."

Sydney about jumped out of her skin. "Hey!" She placed a hand over her heart, "You scared me."

"My bad."

"No problem." She took a deep breath to settle her racing heart. But looking at him increased it, a notch or two. "How was our nap?"

"Amazing. I didn't realize how tired I was. Join me." He patted the cushion beside him.

Sydney walked across the room. The soft glow from the moon and the light in the bathroom lit the room enough to see his figure on the couch. She approached, and the details of his face became much clearer. He casually draped an arm over the back of the couch and shifted turning his body towards her.

"I think we should talk." She could feel his breath on the side of her neck. He placed a soft kiss at the base sending a chill through her body.

"About what?"

He pulled back placing a finger under her chin. "Us."

This conversation was necessary, but she couldn't trust her voice. Not with feeling his firm body against hers.

"I'm listening."

"You're driving me insane woman." His smile turned into a strained chuckle. "I walk into RSE, and I smell your perfume. I visit the studio, and I hear your voice. It's like you're everywhere but where I want you the most."

"And where's that Cameron?"

"Beside me, with me, beneath me…." He accented each position with a pillow soft kiss on her lips.

"What about my contract?" She looked up into his eyes, and raging need stared back. The heat in his eyes made her insides melt.

"We'll leave RSE at RSE. This is about us."

Sydney climbed on his lap straddling his body, letting the white fabric cascade around him. "I'm not too heavy am I?"

"Not at all." His large hands massaged her back then gripped her butt. His mouth kissed between the valley of her breast, he brushed back the lapel of the robe and his eyes triple in size. "Where are your clothes woman?"

Sydney laughed, "In the bedroom. Should I put them back on?"

"Hell nah!"

Cameron lowered the robe off her shoulders with his eyes surveying her naked body. His scorching gaze made her cover her breasts with an arm by reflex.

"Oh no, you don't baby." He peeled her arm away and latched on to her bud. He cupped the underside, suckling one and teasing the other until her nipples were rock hard. She gripped his head closer as he feasted like a starving man.

She gripped the back of the couch and rocked her body closer. He shifted beneath her rubbing his manhood against the source of her agony. He wasn't the only one going insane.

From the moment they crossed paths at S&J, he was all she could think about. His intense gaze fueled every word she sung in the booth. A delicious shudder shot through her at the thought of knowing she'd finally have what she'd craved, what she wanted, *Cameron Carter*.

He pulled back, their lips met in a wet and heated explosion. She gripped his ears, nibbling on his full lips. He palmed her butt and press their bodies together. The only thing separating them was his pants. She slipped her hands between them and grabbed his thick bulge.

His eyes rolled back. "Are you ready for this baby?"

"I've wanted this since the moment I saw you."

He flipped her over on her back with the strength of ten men. Not phased by her fuller body and she wrapped her thick legs around his waist.

"You don't want it more than I do." He said, as his body heat seeped into hers. She scrambled to unbutton his shirt, buttons flying everywhere. He removed his shirt, and she reached for his belt.

"Let's take this to the room."

CAMERON SCOOPED HER UP AND COVERED THE DISTANCE TO her room without thought. He had a very naked Sydney in his arms, and in moments he planned to be deep inside the warmth of her body.

"I can walk."

"This is much faster."

He lowered her to the bed. Lust burned his brain, and he could think of nothing else. Nothing but her sweet, forbidden body. He'd take his time and pleasure every inch of her. Keeping women at a distance made this moment worth the wait.

Urgent with need Cameron tossed his wallet on the nightstand after removing the protection. He stood at the end of the bed. A replay of his nightly dream about her unfolded before him.

"Unbraid your hair."

He unbuckled his belt, then his pants as Sydney rustled her hands through her thick brown hair. His pulse quickened as she leaned back against the pillows. His johnson pointing them in the right direction.

"Take off the robe."

He'd never seen a more beautiful sight. Her body twisted and turned on the bed, hot and ready for him. Her hands gripped her full breast.

"That's for me to do." He climbed in the bed as it buckled under his weight. He trailed his tongue up the length of her leg. Nibbling behind her knee. He kissed his way up her thighs, settling his shoulders behind her luscious thighs. He inhaled, the sweet aroma let him know she was ready.

"Cameron."

His thumbs parted the wet folds of her flesh, she gasped, and his tongue began an intimate quest. He teased, suckled, and licked until he felt her legs quiver. But his mouth didn't stop, couldn't stop. Knowing he could inflict a little of the torture he'd experience since Austin was enough to make him burst.

She pleaded with him to fill her, but not yet. Her

sounds only fed his need to please her. And with every whisper, every moan, every gasp she made herself his.

Then he heard the shift in her pants, sucking for air, gripping the back of his head. A firm thrust of his tongue sent her over the edge. Her cry of pleasure sounded like a melody made just for him.

CHAPTER ELEVEN

*R*aw, wild need passed between them.

Cameron's body prowled against hers in the darkness. He didn't need light to know every inch of her body. His hands traced the curves of her body, soft behind his curious fingers. He held the condom between them, and her golden eyes flashed in the dark.

She ripped it open with her teeth, and he felt her hot little hands slide it down over his shaft. Then she guided him to her core, placing the tip of his head at the door of her sweetness. He teased her, playing at the door waiting for her to let him in.

"Are you seducing me, Mr. Carter?"

"No love, I'm loving you." He pushed his thickness into her softness. Her legs opened wider, and he pressed deeper in long slow strokes as her cries of pleasure threatened to cut their session short.

They moved together as one.

Sydney dug her nails into his back as she held on for

this sweet ride, filling her completely. He pinned her hands above her head and rode her like their lives depended on it. Her soft body pent beneath his rock hard chest and abs. This was worth the wait.

She could see the stars twinkling behind her eyes. It didn't stop her from whispering for more as his passionate grunts mingled with her moans.

"Cameron…baby…"

"Let me hear you sing…."

And she did, a hoarse cry from the depth of her soul erupted, pleasure exploded robbing her of every thought but him. She felt his body tense then an animalistic grunt showered over them.

He tumbled to her side pulling her body against his.

He'd just made her his.

CHAPTER TWELVE

*S*ydney laid awake as he slept soundly beside her. Don't get your hopes up. Enjoy it for what it is. *You're just having a good time.* None of this line of dialogue was helping her. He ravished her body all night. And while he slept like a baby, she was a mess.

The last five years she spent getting to know herself. And what she knew more than anything was she had a bad habit of clinging to people. It wasn't her proudest moment. But it was something that made clinging to music, clinging to drugs, clinging to no good men easy. Even when it resulted in a disaster.

Did clinging to good men count? *Yes!!!* Clinging to good men was worse than the bad ones. The good ones made it harder to let go. To separate physical pleasure from her heart.

Man was she a wreck.

"Do you prefer Sydney or Lady Bird?" He said out of nowhere.

"You're up?"

He nodded and chuckled at her. "Yes."

"How long have you been awake?"

"Long enough to hear you talking to yourself." He smiled and chuckled.

She playfully smacked his chest. "That's not nice Cameron."

"Talk to me, baby."

"I promise you don't want to hear the craziness going on inside my head."

"Actually, I do." He opened his eyes and the sincerity she saw made her reach over and kiss him. He pulled her head to his shoulder and kissed her forehead.

"What do you want to know?"

CAMERON THOUGHT ABOUT HER QUESTION. HE WANTED TO know everything. Anything to help him piece together the moment it happened. That she'd wiggled her way past his defenses or the moment he'd willingly let her in. Because right now, it didn't get much better than this.

Not music, not inking another deal, and it overwhelmed him. She evoked reds, greens, and yellows in his head. And no one had *ever* done that before.

"Do you prefer Sydney or Lady Bird?"

"It depends. The choice is more like Sydney and Bird. Bird was a family nickname. My mom called me her baby bird. She said I would sit and rock singing like a bird perched on a limb." She smiled. "She'd sing, baby bird, baby bird sitting in a tree, S-I-N-G-I-N-G." Her words drifted off. "And when Isaac came along it was easier to say Bird than Sydney."

"You don't have to continue."

"No, it's okay. I haven't given it much thought. I've been so focused on running from my past that I left the good times behind with the bad."

"What are you running from?" She shivered in his arms. Cameron pulled her closer, placing a kiss on her lips. He whispered, "Tell me Bird."

"That night." Her voice broke, and his heart ached.

"Come here baby, I got you." He pulled her to his chest sending all the love he could to her. He'd searched online. In the end, he refused to read the articles, watch the videos, or entertain the opinions of gossip blogs. "You don't have to talk about it."

"No, I want you to hear it from me. But I can't do it press against your chest." Her determination showed in her iron straight back. She leaned over and kissed him, he slipped her a little tongue to make her moan then covered her hands with his.

"I told you about LA. I became a regular at several clubs and open mics. I wasn't aiming to get signed, I just liked the cash payouts for the winners. After winning for several months, I was approached by One Time."

"Diesel Armstrong of Southern Sounds?" He asked with deceptive calm. They'd crossed paths a few times. Cameron didn't like that dude.

"Yes. He started popping up at every show. Then he started sending flowers and expensive gifts. I avoided him for months then he told me about Southern Sounds and offered me a deal."

Cameron tensed, One Time had been blown away by her too. A feeling of jealousy rioted in him.

"You good?" She squeezed his hand.

"Yes, please continue."

"I thought he was blowing smoke. I continued to ignore him until he showed up one night with a check for $10,000." She looked over at him. "I'd never seen a check with a comma, let alone, five figures." She shook her head in disbelief. "I was living in a slum apartment in LA barely making ends meet, working two jobs and singing almost nightly just to have dust in my bank account. And he gives me ten stacks."

"So you signed with Southern Sounds?"

"I did. I signed, and my entire life changed. I was moved to a condo, he bought me a Benz, took me on shopping sprees. I should have known." She whispered the last part more to herself than him.

"Known what?"

"That there was a catch. It was too good to be true. Who was I to come from a small town to the big city and get swept away in La La Land. It was like he smelled my insecurity."

"What happened next?"

She laid back next to him, wiggling closer. "The album, then tours, and more money than I'd made in my life. I traveled the world and didn't see any of it. Nothing but the inside of stadiums and hotels."

He planned to change that. She would see the world if he could help it.

"Then management started stacking my shows. I'd have pre-recorded talk shows during the day and concerts at night. Then we'd record on the tour bus in between. Once I recall 72 hours of nonstop *stuff*." She laid so still and quiet. What was she thinking? "One night before a show I was so exhausted. I couldn't keep my eyes open. One Time gave me a pill, said it was like an Emergen-C and coffee mixed. It would help me feel better."

She rolled over on her back. "It quickly became stimulants to perk me up. Downers to help me sleep. Weed to help me relax. Ecstasy to turn me on. I was taking whatever they gave me. And they gave me anything to keep me on stage. To keep me singing. And Cam, I was miserable. It was like a runaway train heading straight towards me, and I had no way to stop it, and I couldn't move."

He didn't know what to say. He wrapped an arm around her. "Where was Isaac? And your family?"

"Isaac was a kid back home, and my parents were somewhere strung out. I was sending money home to them not knowing I was feeding their addictions." She sat up again. "That night I'd had enough. I felt so alone, yet I was surrounded by people. Half of them I didn't even know. All of them living off my voice." A shadow of rage crossed her face. "I told One Time. And he pushed and pushed. He asked if I wanted to go back to Kansas City and be a nobody. Said no one would listen to my music. That the only thing I had going for me was my voice."

A chill black silence surrounded them. Cameron never in wanted to hurt a human being the way he wanted to get his hands on One Time. The man was known as a shady manager but hearing what Sydney experienced just placed him at the top of Cameron's shit-list.

"CAN YOU IMAGINE HAVING ALL THAT SUCCESS AND FEELING miserable day and night? I wanted to die. So I took speed-ball." Sydney shrugged. "It was a mixture of morphine and cocaine my body rejected it. I was dead on my feet, and you wanna know what he did?" She looked over at Cameron, tears rolling down her cheeks, terrible regrets assailed her. "He had them set up a stool and pushed me out on the stage. Because the show had to go on."

She didn't value her life, her gift. She just wanted it to end. To make it all stop. "I died that night. But I had enough sense to pray. I prayed harder than I'd ever prayed. I begged God to remove me from that situation." She felt Cameron's strong arms around her, she swallowed hard, "They brought me back to life and before One Time could come and get me, I got in my car with the clothes on my back and left LA. I never returned."

Cameron sat so quiet, so still. Should she leave? Would he void her contract? No one knew the whole story. Embarrassment made her keep it to herself, besides most people didn't care...until now.

"I'm better now Cam—"

"Shh...baby." He kissed her, she swore beams of love were dropped into her tattered soul. Her eyes remained open wondering what he'd do now that he knew. Cameron pulled them back to the bed. "Thank you for trusting me enough to tell me. You're amazing."

"You're not going to cancel my contract?" Shocked, she searched his eyes in the shadow of the dark room.

"No." He sounded offended. "But I will extend the option to void the contract with no penalty or consequences."

"Why?" Her voice raised an octave.

"Your response to my offer makes total sense. I don't want you to feel pressured into our agreement. I didn't know."

Sydney brushed away her tears, glad to finally get it off her chest. She was ready to move on for good. "No, sir. You are not getting rid of me."

"What?"

"You came with your offer right on time. I needed to experience RSE to see that not all contracts were like Southern Sounds and not all men are like One Time. You gave me back my first love. I have music again, and it's all because of you Cameron."

"My offer stands."

"Well, get ready for it to remain untouched. I'm officially a member of the RSE family."

"You have no idea what you're agreeing to," he chuckled.

"I think I have a pretty good idea." She smiled happy to have told Cameron the full story. "And Cameron, I'm clean. All of my results are in my phone. I can show you.

And I haven't used drugs or drank alcohol since that night."

"That's why you left S&J so fast?"

"Yes, I don't go to clubs. That was my first night on a stage in five years."

"You looked like an old pro."

"I was sort of amazing." She rolled over to her stomach and kissed his chest. "And I met this fiiiine chocolate brother. You might know him."

Cameron's laughter filled the room pushing out all the bad energy.

"Now that you know all my dark secrets, and all my shortcomings, do you think it's possible to feed me?"

"I think I can handle that, after dessert." His eyebrows wiggle and Sydney was a goner.

CHAPTER THIRTEEN

"*C*ereal is not *real* food." Sydney shoveled the Cheerios into her mouth, in her pink bunny onesie.

"Cooking is not my thing, and you've said no restaurants. So, Your Highness, cereal and sandwiches are on the menu." They sat on the deck watching the morning surfers. Sydney had a smile permanently glued to her face. Which meant all was right in his world.

They went out shopping at the area boutiques yesterday. Then came back to hang out around the pool. Today, she asked to do "absolutely nothing," and he planned to grant her wish.

"I'll throw in a pizza if I get to see you in that bikini again." He loved her body. He wondered if he'd ever tire of being inside her.

"I'll let you see me in my *birthday suit* if you go get some groceries."

Cameron jumped up. "I'll be back."

Her infectious laugh followed him in the house. Cameron threw on some jeans and a t-shirt. He grabbed his keys and jotted her list in his phone. Yesterday they only grabbed the necessities—clothes and stuff to survive. But he'd go to the galaxy and bring back the moon if she asked.

Cameron smacked her delicious tush and went to find his baby some food.

He drove to the area market pondering all Sydney revealed. He reasoned that she needed a fresh start without the dark cloud of Southern Sounds hanging over her head. And only one person stood in the way of having her beautiful voice on his soundtrack, and that was One Time.

He rushed around the store grabbing everything on her grocery list. He jumped in his car, and before he locked his seatbelt, he pressed Damian's number and left a message.

"Yo, Damian, I need The Shark, like yesterday. Meet me in the office Monday at 10."

SYDNEY SEARCHED THE KITCHEN FOR A SKILLET AND A PAN. She placed them on the island and washed her hands. Cameron walked in with a handful of plastic bags.

"Wash your hands."

She set up the food on the island.

"What do you want me to do?" He asked with a smile on his handsome face.

"You pick, cook the ground meat or cut the vegetables for the salad."

"I'll take the meat."

"So, I bared my soul last night," she glanced up from cutting the tomato, "are ready to tell me about her?"

He froze. "Her who?"

"The woman who broke your heart."

He went back to cooking the meat.

"I write love songs. I know the signs. You have a fine man. All his friends and brothers are booed up, having babies, and he's out being a man whore."

"Man whore? I think I'm offended." Teasing laughter reflected in his eyes.

"I didn't call *you* a man whore, but if the shoe fits." She grabbed the onion and went to work.

"Her name is Gabrielle, and for the record, I don't think she broke my heart. It was more of a pride thing." She stopped and glanced over at him. His back was to her as he chopped at the meat in the skillet with extra force. She quickly washed her hands and wrapped her arms around him, resting her head on his back, enjoying the feel of his strong back muscles as he moved. He kissed her hand.

"We dated for a while in high school then connected again in college, dating my junior and senior year." She felt him shrug. "She always wanted to hang out at my family gatherings. She jumped at concerts and any opportunity to attend industry parties."

"Industry parties?"

"Yeah, my father is a member of the *Sin*Sations."

"I forgot about that."

"...lady, I'd die for a drop of your love..." He sang.

"You sing?" She glanced around him.

"Not like you or Marques. But the apple didn't fall too far from the tree."

"Why am I just learning this?"

"It's not my thing. I prefer the business side. I'll leave the stage to the professionals."

"Right." She leaned back against him shocked. Cameron had a warm tenor, no, it was a baritone voice. Wonders never cease.

"I guess looking back I see the signs. It was always about being seen in public with a Carter." She could hear the distaste in his voice.

"That must suck."

"I was used to it. That's why I valued my friendships with Damian and Bruce so much. It was never about our parents. And I thought she was a real one."

"So what happened?"

"How's this?" He leaned to the side for her to check the ground meat.

"Not bad. I might be able to teach you a thing or two. Grab those two cans."

He brought the sauce over then sat at the island. "Towards the end of our senior year. I had peeped her game and planned to break it off. Then she came crying about her ex-having a videotape of them having sex. He wanted five thousand dollars for the tape."

"And like a good boyfriend, you helped."

"I did, only to find out it was a lie. There was no

tape." He started off into the distance. "People don't realize my parents are wealthy not us. Five thousand dollars to a college student was a lot of money, and I didn't want to go to my parents to get it."

"What did you do?"

"I went to my friends. We pulled our money and bought the 'tape.'" He air quoted. "I felt foolish for not seeing her coming. Then to pull my friends into the situation."

"Did you ever tell your parents?"

"No. I hate that people always saw us as a way to get to their money. Totally disregarding how hard my parents work to amass their estate. My father still tours and does shows. My mother fundraises for charities. My parents are amazing people, you'll meet them at the picnic, but to dwindle them down to their bank account is inhumane and disappointing."

She would meet his parents, a warm sensation filled her heart, he saw a future with her.

"And then the man-whoring began." She smiled, wanting him to join her.

"Enough with the man whoring." He landed a loud kiss on her cheek with a smack and snuggled up behind her. "Okay, so a little bit of manwhoring went down. They dubbed me *Playboy Carter*."

"I knew it!" They laughed.

"I'm a good looking, wealthy, black male. I had my choice of women. So, I did." He examined his voice, not boasting or bragging.

"Is that how you see us?" Her voice dropped.

He turned her around. "No, which is why I'm sharing this story with you. I want to see where we go. I'm feeling you, and I know you're feeling me." He rubbed against her.

Sydney rolled her eyes. "I mean you are a good looking, wealthy, fiiiine *chocolate* brotha—"

"You're a mess."

They cooked lasagna and talked about music, sports, and life. By the close of the night, she was cuddled in his arms not ready to return to Houston. She hoped what they'd found this weekend wasn't left on the island.

"Cam."

"Yeah, baby what's up?"

She turned in his arms. "So the after-hours rule is out, right?"

"Yeah, baby. Stop worrying so much. I got you. But I do recall you mentioning a birthday suit." He smacked her butt.

"After stuffing my face with lasagna you want to see me naked?" This man loved her curvy body, and she was down for it.

"I will *always* vote for the birthday suit." She laughed until she cried.

"Cleaning house…"

"Birthday suit, see I can pull up behind you and…." He wiggled against her backside.

"Cooking…"

"Birthday suit, I can place your sexy ass on the table, spread your sweet thighs, and devour—"

"Cameron!"

"You asked. The kitchen is the perfect place for *dessert*." He wiggled his mischievous brows and kissed her softly. He laid back closing his eyes as if drooped closed. *Not yet oh man of mine.*

"And what about now," she straddled him, loving the feel of his thick flesh growing between them.

"I want you butt-ass naked." His mouth joked, but when his eyes opened the sensual blaze, she witnessed made her reach for the hem of her shirt. She pulled it over her head and tossed it across the room. She reached for his shirt, Cameron lifted his body, and she eased it over his head. It soon landed next to hers.

She lowered her mouth fluttering kisses across his broad chest, swirling her tongue around his nipple, raking her nails down his chest. "Did you get more condoms?"

"No doubt." His gruff response made her core throb in need.

They were heading back to Houston. But Cameron was scheduled to leave on Tuesday. She missed him already. She continued her tour of his body as a lusty feeling of heat stole over her. The fullness of his manhood made her mouth water. She hooked her fingers around the waistband of his boxers and exposed him. He was ready.

"Syd…"

Cameron gripped the back of her head as she wrapped her sweet little hands around the base of his erection, lingering at the tip before slipping him into the warmth of her mouth. Her coaxing tongue, the gentle hum vibrating through his body, her steady rhythm, all of it was driving him mad. He fought his release but then she grabbed his jewels, and the sweet suction of her mouth was too much.

"*Fuck* Syd..."

She sat back on the heels of her feet, licked her lips and a pleased look spread across her face. He'd never wanted to be inside a woman so bad. He pent her to the bed, covered himself and seared into her. Branding her. Making her his, and only his.

He sat them up, missing her mouth. He slowed the pace knowing this would have to hold her over until he returned. He wanted her to miss him. To need him. To love him.

The barriers he'd lived behind no longer existed. She'd slipped past and now resided in a dark and dusty place. A place he'd closed off from the world. But Sydney and her luscious body, powerful voice and resilient spirit had kicked it down, and it crumbled beneath her feet, leaving him exposed.

He felt her walls tighten around him. He gripped her hips as she rode him like a Texas cowgirl. Each thrust bringing them closer to paradise.

He tangled his hands in her hair, "Open for me."

Sydney did without hesitation. They kissed open-mouthed, panting as he rocked her body into submission. His sweet words assuring her that he was hers and she was his. Kissing away all doubt and fear. Her body bowed to his probing, his touch, his loving. And when she climaxed it ripped through her body like lightning.

"Cameron!"

Her body jerked, and his rocking increased. She was about to come again. A soul shattering orgasm sent her over the edge. Nothing compared. Her addictive nature latched on to the euphoria and knew she couldn't let him go.

He tensed beneath her and growled into the darkness of the night. "Damn girl, what are you doing to me?"

Falling in love with you. There was no coming back from this.

CHAPTER FOURTEEN

*C*ameron left Sydney at her place. They needed to find her a long-term housing option. He returned to meet with Damian before leaving for LA with Bruce.

"Knock, knock." Eliana's head peeping around the corner. "Got a second."

"Sure." He set his briefcase on the floor and removed his jacket. He settled behind his desk turning on his computer.

"I have your schedule." She passed it across the desk. They'd tried to move her to A&R, but it didn't work. Her role now served as a crazy hybrid between all RSE departments. "Let's start with page two, your most important meeting."

He nodded, flipping through the document. "Shoot."

"The bulk of your time will be with Rashan and his team. He makes it appear pretty seamless. Basically, just wow the other movie producers."

"Do we need to take anything other than our treatment and the demo?"

"No, but I'd suggest taking a few extras for the movie cast. That way Bruce can potentially meet with them while you're out there. It might save you an extra trip."

"I like the sound of that. Schedule studio time while we're out there. Bruce's preferred locations are—"

"On the cloud, I'll take care of it." She talked through the rest of his plans and accommodations.

He was traveling on their private plane and should return by early next week. He wouldn't see Sydney for an entire week. The desire to stop by her place and see her again rushed over him. He glanced at his watch, but time wasn't on his side.

"Cameron, are you listening?" He glanced up to see Eliana's cross face.

"I apologize." He didn't hear anything beyond the duration of his trip.

"Y'all must be done hiding."

He lowered the document. "Come again?"

"You and Sydney thought you had somebody fooled." She sat back in the chair, her eyes dancing with excitement. "I knew it."

"Knew what?" Damian stepped in without knocking.

"That Sydney and Cameron have a thing going on." They shared a smile.

"Oh really, do tell," Damian said, sitting next to her.

Cameron barely heard their exchange. He thought they hid it well, now everyone will know.

Does that bother him? No, it didn't. He wanted everyone to know she was off the market and all his.

"Playboy Carter falling for an R&B Bad Girl. That has an interesting ring to it." Damian teased.

"I will keep my comments to myself." Cameron declared, but he had no room to talk. "But for the record, your wife is a saint."

"I know."

They laughed. Eliana stood to leave them alone.

"Can you schedule to meet with Damian while I'm gone? Sydney needs long-term housing. She's been in the hotel for a month. I think we can do better than that."

"I'm on it boss." And with a wave, she was off.

He turned to Damian. "Thanks for coming. How's the fam?"

"Growing." He chuckled. "The baby is due soon, and the center is expanding."

"You need to let that woman breathe." This was baby number two in less than three years.

"Man, I tried. I can't keep my hands off her."

Cameron laughed until his eyes filled with unshed tears. "I don't blame you."

"What, no jokes? So, your thing with Sydney is true?"

"Man," Cameron sat back. "I think one of y'all added a potion to the water because...." He didn't have words for it.

"This is serious." Damian moved to the edge of the chair.

"Yeah man, it's serious."

"And you're ready to give up your player ways?" His eyebrows shot up in surprise.

"No doubt. She's it."

"It? As in, wifey?" His smile widened in approval.

Cameron nodded and chuckled at the stunned Damian. "But there seems to be an issue with a previously signed recording contract."

He sat back, all traces of humor gone. "Start at the top."

For the next hour, he walked Damian through the happenings from the showcase at S&J to last night. Not everything, but all the pertinent details. Damian asked a million questions as usual without taking a single note.

"Dude you are really a scary creature." Cameron joked.

"That's why you keep me around." He tossed back standing. "I'll do some digging. How far do you want me to go back?"

"I want to know from the moment his father shot up the club." Cameron leaned forward. "And do some searching on Southern Sounds. Their parent company, distribution, artists. And any other angles that will remove this asshole from Sydney's life, for good."

"Do you think he'll come after her?"

"Not and live." His gut twisted at the thought of harm coming her way. They had around the clock security and cameras on the premises.

"Calm down Romeo. He obviously was trying to blacklist her. Learning she has a contract with RSE won't be good news."

Cameron dropped his head back, her safety came first. "Let's switch out her driver for one of our armed bodyguards. And I'll talk with her about assigning her a bodyguard until we get this matter under control."

"That sounds good. I'm on it." Damian stood.

"And thanks, man." He stepped around his desk and hugged his friend. Glad to have him on their side.

"You'd do the same for me and mine. And don't worry, the man may be reckless but he ain't crazy."

"Yeah, I hope not."

"I'm out." Damian strolled to the door.

"Family…"

"Over fame."

Cameron sat on the edge of his desk. He dropped his head to his chest and prayed for Sydney. He reached across his desk and picked up his cellphone. He scrolled through his history and tapped her contact.

"Hello." Her groggy voice made him smile.

"Mind if I stop by before I head to the airport."

"Not at all, I'll be waiting in my birthday suit." She giggled.

"I plan to break every moving violation in the State of Texas to get to you girl."

"And I'll be waiting. But make it here in one piece."

"No doubt."

He disconnected the line and grabbed his briefcase. He knew digging could rouse One Time, but the sooner they ironed out this mess, the sooner *they* could move on.

SYDNEY ARRIVED AT RSE WITH A PLANNED APOLOGY FOR Bruce. She acted like a brat. And she knew it after hearing the final demo with Cameron over the weekend. His suggestions were spot on. She had a lot to learn about teamwork and collaboration. She stepped in the studio to find Marques sitting in Bruce's coveted seat.

"Hey, you!" He stood giving her a hug.

"When did you get back?"

"This morning."

She sat on the couch. "Where's Bruce?"

"You'll work with me while they're in LA. And I'm pretty sure you need a break."

"Boy do I?" She laughed. "We had a huge blow-out Friday."

Marques laughed. "Noooo, what happened?"

She told him all about it. Marques reminded her a lot of Isaac. He had a calming presence about him.

"What do you have planned for me?" She sat forward.

"I have a selfish project." He leaned back in the chair with her full attention. "I want to try to co-write a song together."

"That doesn't sound selfish at all. What do you have in mind?" She reached down into her bag and pulled out her notebook and pen.

"The treatment of the main characters made me think about a couple at odds trying to find their way back to love."

She lowered to the floor in front of the table and jotted down a few notes. "And you want the song to retell their struggle?"

"No, I'm thinking a ballad told from their prospectives. I see the song as a literal bridge between the beginning and end. A bridge they have to cross to make it to the other side."

"Let's do it." She stood and walked over to the board taking the seat beside him. He played a few tracks from Bruce. They agreed on one and went to work.

They ended the night with the melody and the chorus. Cameron texted letting her know he'd made it. He had several meetings but would call her as soon as they had the good news. She sent up a prayer for them.

"You did a great job tonight," Marques said as they prepared to leave.

"Thanks. I'm excited about the progress we've made. I think we could have a finished song by the time they get back." She closed her notebook and walked over to the couch to grab her bag.

"I think so too."

"Mind if I ask you a question?"

"Not at all." He turned facing her.

"How do you do this? You seem to have it all together. Recording, traveling, your family."

"I wish. I just do what Brione says." He laughed.

Sydney mocked writing a note. "Do what Brione says, check."

"No, real talk. Do what she says, and…" he glanced over at her, "there are many factors to success. But for me, it took falling and losing it all to appreciate it. Then I had to fight to get it back."

"What do you mean?"

"I lost my first recording contract."

Sydney combed her mind trying to remember if she knew that piece of information. "Then what happened?"

"It's a long story, but I had to prove to my brothers how bad I wanted my career—to be a full-time artist."

"How did you do it?"

"Much like what they're putting you through. I worked with Bruce for several years. They had to dry me out and build me up. But Sydney, it's worth it. I never ever thought I'd be here." He sat forward. "Actually, I knew I could do it. But my life is so much better than I ever dreamed."

The serene smile on his face said it all.

"How did you learn to trust again?"

"I had it easy there. Cameron made it happen. He left the corporate world and started RSE to back me. I've known Bruce my whole life, and the others for so long that we're family. I already knew and trusted them. But they made me work hard because they knew my potential."

"That's why Bruce is riding my ass?" She joked but was serious too.

"Yep. And the more you grow, the more he'll push. Cameron's the worse. Sydney I'd do it all again. The heartache, the trials, the grueling hours in the studio, the nights on the tour bus. I wouldn't change a moment of it because it led me to this place."

His words intrigued her. Much like leaving the good memories in the past with the bad ones, she now had a fresh perspective for her time with Southern Sounds, it made her contract with RSE possible.

"What about all the vices?" She had no desire to use drugs and drink again. However, she'd never been to an industry event without one or both being present.

"That's a hard one. I would drink and party. Party and drink." His bleak smile spoke volumes. "In the end, I found it wasn't worth it. And it started with changing my surroundings, and having a team that cares about me as a person, not just an artist." His kind eyes bore into her. "Then I was a disaster waiting to happen. Now, I'm a grown man.

"I want to do what I love and provide for my family. I want to get old and love my wife for as long as the good Lord allows. I can't have that with the vices. And anyone that tells you different is a lie."

Marques later walked her out to the waiting car. He told her to call anytime. These RSE men are something. She couldn't wait to meet their parents at the picnic. She half expected them to glide in on wings.

Marques gave her plenty to think about, and on the ride to the hotel, she realized she'd have to learn to balance her self-care with duties as an artist.

As an artist?

She entered her room and slumped to the bed, kicking her shoes off. She had a few hours before Cameron's call. She didn't take this decision lightly. Her sobriety was her number one concern.

Did she really want to be an artist again?

Yes, she wanted it and not just recording an album but performing too.

That meant concerts. Concerts meant traveling. Traveling meant being in situations outside her control. Icy fear twisted in her heart as she crawled into the bed. Her chest felt as if it would burst.

This changes everything.

CHAPTER FIFTEEN

"*H*ot damn! We did it."

Cameron and Bruce stood outside the pristine building with people and cars swooshing by totally unaware of the importance of this moment. They inked the deal.

They hugged and with a few solid pats on Bruce's back they waited for Rashan Carter to join them for lunch.

"Cameron man, you killed that negotiation. Congratulations executive producer."

"The same to you executive producer." Cameron popped his collar with all the swag of a man headed straight for the stars.

"Aaaahhhh!!!" They slapped hands five times, saluted then danced around like kids. "We have to compose ourselves. We're executive producers."

Bruce howled with joy, and Cameron felt the energy rushing through his body. He couldn't wait to tell Sydney. They only had one teeny, weeny, tiny problem: The producers were sold based on Sydney's voice on *Damaged*. They wanted the demos mastered to be the actual songs for the soundtrack. Knowing Marques, a Grammy award-winning artist would sing several songs sweetened the deal.

Cameron glanced back at the glass doors not seeing his cousin yet.

"What are we going to do about Sydney?" Bruce asked.

"Beg."

"Can I watch?" A flash of humor crossed his face. "I think I have a better idea. Because I can't let you go out like that."

They bumped fists as he noticed Rashan coming their way.

"Congratulations!" They danced around like kids again.

"Real talk, thank you for recommending us," Cameron said.

"Thank you for closing on the deal. This is a win for all of us."

Cameron nodded. It was. They'd worked years of developing Marques, then building RSE's reputation in the industry. Now, it was time to expand. It was all coming together.

"Let's get out of here, I'm starving."

THEY WENT TO A SWANK BEVERLY HILLS RESTAURANT AND talked about a few additional details. Cameron glanced out the window thinking about the LA Sydney experienced. She left in a cloud of scandal but would return with her voice narrating a major motion picture with an A-list cast.

Cameron and Bruce went their separate ways and planned to reconnect later tonight for a mixer with Rashan and the cast. He showered and changed suits. He glanced at his watch, he wanted to give Sydney time to sleep.

His phone rang. He had a FaceTime call coming in.

"Hey, gorgeous." He sat on the edge of the bed.

"Hey yourself handsome. Don't you look tasty."

"Well, what can I say?" They laughed. "How did your session with Marques go?"

"It was amazing!"

"Amazing? Tell me all about it."

He walked to the couch propping his phone on the arm. He sat back loving the sound of her voice. She told him about their writing session and his great advice.

"I'm glad you two connected. I think you can both help each other. You have many shared experiences. And it should make for wonderful music." He smiled, wishing he could touch her.

"He helped me realize something." The somber tone caught his attention.

"And what's that?"

"I want to sing again." His heart jumped to his throat.

"What brought this on?" He watched the emotions dance across her face, excitement, fear, dread, determination, all in seconds.

"My life without music is like a piece of my soul is missing. And frankly, I'm tired of hiding. I'm working hard on this soundtrack, and I want to experience it all."

"Baby, I'm glad you've come to this decision because the producers loved you."

"They did?"

"They did. And one day you'll stop being surprised by the spell you've cast over us."

"I'm not casting a spell. I'm just doing what I love."

"So, you're saying I got you for the soundtrack?" He held his breath.

"Well, it depends." She pulled her bottom lip between her teeth.

"Woman, don't do this to me. I have a meeting, and I can't focus when you look at me like that."

"Fine. You got me." She laughed. "But what about my contract with Southern Sounds?"

"I'm looking into it." Relieved he sat back and talked with her until it was time to head out. "Look babe, I gotta run. We're meeting with the cast tonight."

"Alright, no man whoring. *Playboy Carter* is officially out of business." Joy bubbled in her laugh and shone in her golden eyes. He could get used to her.

"Man, what I tell you about that? Besides, my woman holds it down."

"Damn right," she teased. "Hey, Cam…"

"What's up, baby?" He leaned closer as if he could touch her through the screen.

"I'm your woman?"

"Damn right." She was unlocking a different side of him. And he liked it. "Bye babe."

"Bye Cam."

They held the line. He had to hear her laugh one more time.

"Hey, Syd?"

"What's up, baby?" Her lips twitched with the need to smile.

"Can I call you later?"

"Damn right!"

They talked for a while longer, neither wanting to end the call. His side hurt from laughing. She was heading to volunteer at Harmony, and he was off to mingle with the cast, counting down the minutes until she was in his arms again.

"How was Harmony?" He stretched out in the bed with his iPad propped on a pillow.

"I just love going to Harmony Dance." She held her hands to her heart with a smile on her face.

"Tell me about it." And this was how their week went. They talked between his meetings, after her sessions, squeezing in text messages and video calls.

"Today I met with the RSE wives. We worked on the picnic arrangements." She sat on the bed with her legs crossed braiding her hair.

"What are you in charge of?" The ladies rotated duties over the years.

"Food."

"Food? Are you ready for that?"

"Do you doubt me?" Her eyebrow spiked daring him to say the wrong thing.

"Nah baby it just that the RSE family is serious about their food."

"So am I? Don't you see these hips." She slapped one with a smack and went back to braiding.

"I love your hips." She'd mentioned being heavy, her thick thighs, all little subliminal messages causing him to ask. "What's wrong with your hips?"

"Nothing, but if I'm going back to the stage, I need to lose a few pounds."

"Don't you dare." He sat up.

"Cam, you know this industry. We're in the age of bodysuits and fitted clothes. You don't expect me to sing in an evening gown."

"I'm not a stylist, but your music represents freedom and a woman charting her own course. I don't think you should bend to the norm. Be yourself."

"So you don't mind my extra pounds?"

"Did I not taste every inch of your body?"

"Cam…"

"I had your thick thighs wrapped around my neck." He cupped his hands. "And your perfect a—"

"Okay, Cameron." Her cheeks flushed with color. "You like my body."

"I *love* your body."

"You love my body." She laid on her stomach closer to the camera, "I love your body too."

"All jokes aside," he picked up his iPad bringing her near, "I get that people make comparisons. But what about the little girl excited to see a plus-size woman with full natural breast and full curves rocking out on the stage. Not taking away from the other women. But there's a space just for Sydney Jones. I say walk in it."

"I've been thinking about keeping you around, you're good for a woman's ego."

He chuckled. "I got you. But what's in it for me?" He wiggled his eyebrows.

"I can't talk to you with that silly look on your face." She giggled.

"I'm serious. What's in it for me? I gas you up, you gotta have something for yo boy." He leaned back, smiling. This Syd would have him on the line all night until he had her in his arms.

"How about…a lifetime supply of birthday suit vouchers?"

"Bet Syd!" Her hands covered her mouth, and she rolled over on her side howling.

"What you want me to say, girl?" He had to yell over her cries for him to stop. Her laughter floated across a thousand miles aimed straight for his heart.

"Girl your hair looks fierce." He said in a falsetto. The more she laughed, the more he cut up.

"And your waist is snatched!" He snapped in an exaggerated fashion.

"And your—"

"Cam…I can't breathe!" She sat up pleading.

"How many vouchers is that Syd?" He laughed

openly as tears streamed down her face. She fell back, flat on the bed holding her stomach, gasping for air. "How many?"

"I love your crazy butt."

It sailed through the air, and his heart snagged it up before she took it back because he loved her too.

CHAPTER SIXTEEN

*S*ydney let the words in her heart tumble out her mouth. First, they were laughing and cutting up, and now she had to focus on her man's face.

Cameron was a man of many colors. He could transition from cool blue to hot red in a blink. His loyalty streak ran deep, and beneath his thick armor, his heart was pure gold.

"Cam, I didn't?"

"You didn't mean it?" Her nerves tensed immediately. She clenched her hands until her nails pierced her palms.

"I meant it. I don't want you to feel obligated to love me back."

The ring of her alarm sounded. She jumped startled. It was time to leave for her session. *Saved by the bell.*

"I gotta go Cam. Talk to you later."

"Syd don't—"

She pressed the red disconnect button on her phone.

She stared at the phone wondering if she ruined it? Had she moved to fast? She saw the exact moment he retreated behind his armor.

She scrambled to her feet to get dressed. The driver would be waiting downstairs. Her phone rung as she pulled the door closed. It was Cameron. She couldn't stand to see that look in his eyes. She turned off her ringer and ignored his call.

Twenty minutes later she rushed from the hotel to the car having ignored five subsequent calls. She had to think of a good response. Thankfully she had until tomorrow to make light of her slip-up.

It wasn't like she said, "I love you." Period.

It was more like, "Boy you so crazy. I love you."

She smacked her palm to her forehead. That sounded stupid and childish, even for talking to herself. She watched the city roll by in a blur until they arrived at the studio.

"Hey Marques, sorry I'm late." She rushed in pulling out her notebook and took the seat beside him.

"No worries." His attention on the knobs and dials, then he looked up. "You good?"

"Yeah." She dropped her head taking extra care with flipping the pages. Dread pooled in the pit of her stomach. She felt like she'd be sick.

"We don't have to do this tonight."

"No," she let out a long audible breath, "I'm ready."

She hoped her smile would convince him. She forced her anxiety aside, focusing on the music. The best way to handle Cameron would come to her.

Sydney told Marques her ideas for the song, praying he'd let it go. She needed the booth tonight. He shot back a few suggestions and sent her to the mic.

Singing would serve as her therapy because regardless of her slip, she loved Cameron. And it was the most thrilling yet scary truth. She loved a man that made her laugh, made her feel safe, and he believed in her. She had to channel her newly acquired status into her music. But letting a man in meant he had the power to throw her life into a tailspin.

She placed the headphones over ears, stepping closer to the microphone.

"Drop the lights."

Marques lowered the lights. It made seeing anything impossible. However, she didn't need the lyrics. They were etched in her heart along with Cameron. She closed her eyes and rocked back and forth, shifting her weight from side to side.

People always wondered how she caused her voice to have such soul. This was how. She lived life, and she didn't hide her truth from her music. The solution was intricately woven into the DNA of her work. It was how she'd survived for so long.

She rolled her shoulders and wiggled her arms trying to relieve the tense energy from her body. Telling her heart, *let love in, let love win.*

"I have the title," she whispered, her eyes darting to him somewhere in the dark. "Let Love Win."

"I like the sound of that Syd."

"Run the track."

"You got it."

The music filled her headphones. *Therapy was in session.*

CHAPTER SEVENTEEN

*C*ameron sat in the hotel frustrated with Sydney for not answering his calls. He called their pilot and bumped their departure time. Bruce didn't question his decision since he had a family waiting at home.

Cameron covered the time and distance thinking of his woman. *I don't want you to feel obligated to love me back.* Obligated to love her? What kind of shit was that?

Love wasn't an obligation. Love wasn't a chore. Love, even when it hurt, was a gift. And despite his feeling about how she handled their conversation, he valued the gift.

"Man, how did you survive all those years loving Sandi from afar?"

"Patience." Bruce chuckled, unaware of the war raging in Cameron. He and his wife were friends for years before Bruce divulged his love for her. "I build a life for us based on hope. Hoping she'd love me the way I loved her. Faith that we'd have this very life I'm living."

The smile on his face was priceless. Bruce and his wife had a bumpy start, suffering several miscarriages. But they never quit on their love.

"I still can't believe I'm married to her. Ain't that a trip." Bruce had a goofy grin on his face. "That I get to go home to her and that she had my children. It is indescribable."

Cameron rested his head against the seat as the plane brought them closer to Houston. "This thing with Sydney has me going mad."

"Spill it."

Cameron glanced out the window into the night. "Everything is right and wrong at the same time. I want her, but the timing couldn't be worse. And she's an artist, *our* artist."

"I need you to use your big boy words." His joking tone lightened the mood. Bruce served as their glue. He was levelheaded yet knew how to go with the flow. "But knowing you since the womb, I have one piece of advice."

"I'm listening."

"Stop trying to control it."

"Control what?" He looked across the aisle at Bruce.

"Everything. That's why it feels right and wrong. How else would it feel right and wrong? Unless you're attempting to dictate what it is or what it should be. Love is a unique beast. You don't choose it. It chooses you. You don't choose the time. You don't choose the person. You don't choose the beginning, *but* you can choose the middle and end."

"Oh wise one, giver of beat and bass, Mr. Lover-Lover,

what should I do?" Cameron smiled, grateful for a friend like Bruce. But he had to pull his leg a bit. Dodging the wad of paper flying in his direction.

"You're an ass sometimes." Bruce laughed.

"Only sometimes?"

"Cameron you have to live in the moment. Sydney's past is not one you expected, but it made her the woman she is today. A strong, resilient woman. The type of woman worthy to be at your side. She's the type of woman men like us need. She's not going to take your shit, and she won't crumble under the pressure of our lives. Like my Sandi."

Sydney was all that and more. Nothing like he expected. She was a constant presence in his mind since the first time he saw her in S&J. Whether she rocked a big wig, she dubbed her stage hair, or a single plait, her beautiful smile, and golden eyes wiggled past his defenses. Past his wall. Past his hurt.

"Do you love her?"

"Yes." He could tell Bruce anything without hesitation. Now, he had to tell Sydney.

"Does she know?"

"No, I wanted to finish this soundtrack and get her Southern Sounds situation under control." Bruce's I-told-you-so eyes met his. Cameron wanted to *control* the situation. He dropped his head telling Bruce about their video call.

"That woman has experience enough. Don't add to it."

Cameron had no words for his friend.

"You asked, how. How could I love Sandi from afar?

I decided to love her whether she wanted my love or not. I would have loved that woman for a lifetime because I knew she was it for me. I decided to pour everything I had into it with no regrets. Not focused on whether she responded in kind, although I knew she would eventually. Her heart loved me, she just didn't know it."

Cameron glanced over at Bruce. *Who is this man?* "I think you need to become our resident love doctor."

"Nah, I know you. That Playboy Carter stuff was your way of avoiding the discord you feel right now. To experience the good you have to make room for the bad. No one is perfect. But if you love her, and she loves you....man it is *heaven*."

No one is perfect, but Sydney was perfect for him.

"I only have one word of caution."

"Tell me oh wise one...."

"Love her or leave her alone."

Bruce laid his head back and promptly went to sleep as Cameron played their conversation over and over in his mind, remixed with her, *I don't want you to feel obligated to love me back*.

He loved her down to his DNA, and it was unlike any previous experiences in his life. It let him know that what he had with Gabrielle wasn't the same. It didn't feel like this.

As the plane descended he gathered his possessions knowing his first stop was RSE. He glanced at his watch, it was a little after four. He still had time. They walked from the plane to their waiting cars.

"Man, I'll see you later." They hugged. "And thank you."

"You're welcome, and for the record, I'm the best man."

"Dude, that's too much. Can I tell the woman I love her first?"

"I got to get my name on the list first." He laughed patting Cameron on the back. "Don't expect to see me for a few days. I need to spend some time with my family." Bruce passed his bags to the driver.

"You should take them to the beach house, Syd and I had a blast."

"I just might do that." He walked to the opened car door. "Where are you heading?"

"To the studio, Syd's session isn't scheduled to end until seven."

"Look," Bruce froze pointing a finger in his direction, "no sex in my chair."

"Who said anything about—"

"*No sex* in my chair."

Cameron laughed, lowering into the car.

"Cameron, I'm serious."

"Bye Bruce."

"Cameron…." He could hear his muffled voice as Cameron closed the car door. He signaled to the driver. "Take me to RSE."

"KID."

Marques jumped glancing over his shoulder. Cameron entered the room like a thief in the night, following the sound of her voice, slipping into the room. It took his eyes a moment to adjust.

"What's up Cam? Are you hearing this?"

"Yeah man." Cameron sat at the board next to Marques. "What song is this?"

"It's a new song we wrote together. It's just about done."

Cameron stood and went back to the couch. He laid back, "Have her run it back."

Marques leaned over the board. "Sydney, let's take it from the top."

"Okay, should I change anything?" Sydney's voice filled the room.

"Don't tell her I'm here," Cameron whispered. The glass partition made it hard to see into the control room when the lights were lowered. It was like a privacy glass meant to help the artist get and stay in the zone.

"No, you're good. I want to get a clean cut from beginning to end. I'll layer my vocals, so add any ad libs or runs."

"Got it."

Marques relaxed in the chair half turned towards the booth, and half in his direction. He pressed a button, and the music dropped.

"Turn it up." The volume increased, and Cameron could feel the under beat vibrating through his body. "What's the title of the song?"

"Let Love Win."

Cameron closed his eyes, waiting for the colors to appear. Marques' hummed over the track and Sydney harmonized with the sweetest twist. He shot up to his feet and glanced at his brother.

"Fire," Marques said.

Cameron listened as their voices played off each other like a conversation between lovers. Fighting for their love. Lobbying for their love. Declaring love the victor over all. He stared at his love in the booth, her words speaking to his heart, drawing him closer, pleading with him. It was as if she wrote the song for him. To him. About them.

Cameron stood the entire song. Frozen. "Kid, we'll see you tomorrow."

Marques glanced over his shoulder and with a pat on Cameron's back he left.

It was time to get a few things straight with his lady.

CHAPTER EIGHTEEN

"*H*ow was that?" Sydney pulled an ear free from the headphones, her heart racing.

"Perfect."

Her heart stopped.

"Cam?" Cupping a hand over her eyes trying to see into the control room. The lights in the booth lifted, and he stood bent over the board. His eyes glued to hers. "Wha…what are you doing here?"

"I work here," he said with an unreadable expression on his face.

"But you weren't scheduled to return until tomorrow," her voice broke falling into a whisper. How long had he been here? Did he hear the entire song? Did he approve?

"I had a change of plans. Come inside."

"No," she shook her head. She wasn't ready for this conversation. She needed more time to make the words work in her favor.

"Syd."

She rocked back and forth, still not convinced. Call her a coward, but after that awesome session, she didn't want to hear anything to kill her high. His brows set in a straight line as if he could read her thoughts.

She watched as he stood upright and turned towards the booth door. *Oh boy, he's coming in here.* She hung the headphones on the stand then rubbed her moist palms on her dress. The door opened, and her man filled the doorway with his broad shoulders. Her eyes floated up to his, he was hiding behind his armor.

"You look tired." She played with her hands, trying to control her nervous energy.

"I've been awake all night." His expression was unreadable.

Knowledge is power. Not now, she thought. *If not, now then when?* Sydney shook her head and heard him chuckle.

"Talk to me, baby."

She glanced up and his eyes brimmed with tenderness. "Baby?"

"Damn right." He closed the door.

Sydney held up her hands like two large stop signs. "I said it. I meant it. But you are under no obligations to say it back. I was caught up in the moment and—"

His mouth was on hers one hand embracing her face the other pulled her body against his. Sydney leaned into his body. He broke the kiss, "I love you Sydney."

"REALLY?" HER EYES GLISTENED WITH UNSHED TEARS.

Cameron's large hands took her face and held it gently, knowing he should have told her sooner. He planned to tell her every chance he got. "Really, I love you Sydney."

He kissed her forehead. "I love you Sydney."

He kissed her nose, then her lips again. "I love you Sydney."

She snaked her arms beneath his and caressed his neck. He lifted her off the ground as her legs wrapped around his waist. He kissed her again, saying the words turned on a flood of emotions. He felt at peace, frustrated, and whole with her. She could bring him to his knees, and she didn't even know it. He walked them back to the padded walls, not removing his lips from hers.

Sydney reached for his belt buckle as he tugged on her panties. Their feverish moves were a blur as he pulled out protection, she slipped it on, and he entered her with urgency.

He arched her on the wall and with each thrust loved her. There were no more words, just the sounds of passion absorbed in the soundproof room. Moving together as one, both giving, both taking, riding the wave of ecstasy. But this was different, rough, primal, welding their souls together.

His groans mingled with her cries as they surrender together.

"I love you too."

CHAPTER NINETEEN

*S*ydney and Cameron settled into a rhythm around the rushed project. For six months they worked around the clock, efficiently recording the soundtrack, as cast members flew in and out of Houston to record their songs.

It was hectic, but it worked.

She'd gone from living at the hotel to staying with Isaac. And now she spent her time split between the studio and Cameron's house. Today, they were finalizing the track sequence before sending the soundtrack off for engineering.

Sydney rolled over and glanced at the clock with a smile on her face. She kissed Cameron's chest. "Babe you up? Babe."

He didn't move a muscle. She rubbed her birthday suit against his and felt Cameron's hand massage her butt. The man could sleep through a hurricane, but the idea of lovemaking could rouse her gentle giant.

"Are you going to Harmony Dance with me?" She propped up on her elbow tracing his lips with a finger.

"For what?" His eyes remained closed.

"I have a taste tasting with the caterer." She gave his body a hearty shake. "Babe, wake up."

"I'm up." He nibbled at her finger, yet didn't open his eyes. "Who's the caterer?"

"Helene's Soul Food Kitchen."

His eyes popped open. "Uncle Jared and Aunt Helene are here?"

"Yep."

"Why didn't you say so?" He stood up and lifted her effortlessly into his arms. Walking through the room to the bathroom cradling her to his chest.

"I tried, but you've been bouncing around the country." He'd traveled scouting new artists. Thank God for video calls. He tried to keep the trips short but a day here and two days there added up. "Where are we going?"

"To shower."

"Oh no, you don't." She tried to wiggle out of his hold. "I will not meet Bruce's parents for the first time with my hair plastered to my head."

"Babe I won't get your hair wet." She rolled her eyes. "Promise."

"I don't believe you for one second Cameron Carter."

"I'll do that thing you like." He nibbled at her ear, and her heart jolted, and pulse pounded.

Would she ever get enough of this devilish man? The answer was an unequivocal, no. He loved her in all the ways a man could and should love a woman. And all was right with her soul with Cameron by her side.

He lowered her to the cold tile floor. She turned on the water. There was no way she wouldn't show up with wet hair, and honestly, she didn't care. Because in about five seconds, she wouldn't know her name.

Sydney smiled as her man kneeled in front of her hoisting her legs over his shoulders. Her overwhelming need for him outweighed reason as her head fell back against the shower wall.

He nuzzled the inside of her thigh. "Bon appetit."

"I LOOK LIKE A WET PUPPY."

They'd arrive at Harmony late thanks to Cameron. He tossed her all through the bathroom, the bedroom, and her hair was plastered to her head. She chuckled.

"I think you look gorgeous." He pinched her nose between his knuckles.

"Thank you. So what's the agenda for today?"

"Are y'all still having the brunch afterward?"

"Yes," she dragged her comb through her hair, plaiting it while Cameron drove.

"I have my class. I bet the guys will be here. So, I'll text them to move the meeting to Harmony. That will save everyone a drive."

She nodded. "I still can't believe we're near the end. What's the status of my contract?"

"Babe, don't get me started."

Damian uncovered the details of her contract a few months ago. They'd made several attempts to locate One Time without success. But knowing One Time, he was waiting to make an entrance.

"I sent out a few feelers in LA. But to be on the safe side, I'm interviewing bodyguards for you."

"Bodyguard? Why do I need a bodyguard?"

"To give your man piece of mind. Will you do that?"

"Yes, Cameron." She leaned over and kissed him.

They pulled up at Harmony Dance. Cameron circled the car to open her door, pulling Sydney up to her feet. His hands, massive and strong, wrapped around her waist. He lowered his mouth to hers, kissing her slow and sweet.

"Thank you," he whispered across her swollen lips. She could kiss him forever.

"Oh, loverboy." A voice called out.

"Marques." They said in unison.

Sydney laughed dropping her head to his chest. "You better get inside before they all come out."

"Yeah, yeah, yeah. They are such pests." He stepped back grabbing her hand, lacing their fingers together.

"And you love it."

His stern face didn't fool her anymore. She'd learned to read him with almost accurate precision, except his colorful forecasts. By her calculation, he had a ninety percent accuracy rate. A few months into her contract she started shadowing Bruce along with Isaac. She saw artists come and go. Many of them singing her songs. And the man would stretch out on the couch and give a yay or nay without a blink or hesitation.

Cameron guided them inside. As always the center was in full force, full of people. Saturdays were the busiest day. Imani had programming for all age levels, children to seniors. Cameron and Marques did their brotherly hug with one arm. Then Marques pecked her cheek.

"Bri here?"

"Yes, her and the kids are back there already."

"Who's all here?" Cameron asked, not letting go of her hand.

"Everyone."

They crossed the lobby going to the back room for the meeting and brunch. They entered the room, and it was like the picnic started today.

"Get ready," Marques whispered down to her, "you're about to meet the folks."

Sydney halted, shocked.

"Don't worry."

"Just be prepared for Pops to flirt with you." Marques joked, Cameron groaned.

Sydney shook her head, she'd also learned to stay out of their brotherly teasing.

"Uncle Cam!" A voice screeched from across the room.

He dropped Sydney's hand just in time to catch a little girl. "Hey, Sweetheart! When did you get back?"

"This morning." He hugged her tight, twisting back and forth. "I missed you."

"I missed you more. Kayla, I'd like to introduce you to

Miss Sydney." Kayla glanced over her shoulder as Cameron lowered her to the ground. "Miss Sydney this is my lovely niece, Kayla."

"Hi," she smiled, holding on to Cameron's hand, "nice to meet you."

"Nice to meet you too." Sydney returned her smile, she looked exactly like her mother.

"Which way is your Mom?"

"Over there." She pointed to the far wall.

"I'll let you two catch up." Cameron nodded.

Sydney headed to the table with the wives, stepping around kids and toys. She stopped to hug little ones here and there. And the guys, here and there too. It looked like the entire RSE family was in one room.

"Hey!" She gave an exaggerated wave to the ladies.

"It's time to get you officially broken into the family. You will get the *entire* tea today." Imani said. "Let me point everyone out. There is the Daniels family, the Hughes family, and the Carters."

Sydney couldn't keep up with all the names. Isaac found her a while later sitting marveling at the grandness of the bunch.

"This is something, ain't it?" He kissed her cheek and sat beside her.

"It is. Just when I get used to their family dynamic, it gets more complexed."

"I was like that for the first few years." He laughed.

"But now you fit right in." She looked over at her brother.

"Pretty much. I don't get names mixed up anymore. And if I miss a family function, I get chewed out. So, yeah, I guess it's official."

"What should I expect from the Carters?" She leaned into his side.

"Besides Pops being a flirt, they're good people. Mrs. Michelle would give you the shirt off her back. Mr. Curtis is the life of the party." He glanced down at her, "Don't worry, they'll love you."

"How did you get used to all of this?"

"I felt weird at first. They love hugging, and staying connected. I thought it was an act. No family could possibly be this close, but now, I'm a believer. It's like this at every holiday."

"Wow!"

"I know."

To think it was the two of them. Their mother died from an overdose, and their father followed not too long after. That's what scared her straight. If she died, it would leave Isaac alone, and she never wanted to do that to him. They were all they had. Until now.

"You and Cam still good."

"We're great. I'm concerned about this contract though. They can't find One Time." She felt Cameron's eyes on her and scanned the room until she found him. *I'm fine*, she mouthed, and he went back to rolling around on the floor with the twins. "Cameron wants to hire a bodyguard."

"*Good*. One Time is ignorant. I wouldn't put anything

past him. And I have this for you." He passed her a set of keys. "I know you don't need them but just in case. We're heading out for a few shows before the school year starts. Mi casa is su casa. Although I doubt you'll need them."

"Thanks." She dropped them in her purse. "Do you need me to check on anything while you're away?"

"If you could grab my mail a couple times a week… that would help." His tone had become chilly.

"Done." She looked in the direction of his gaze with the sea of people it was hard to pinpoint the exact person. But she had an idea. "So what's up with you and Eliana?"

"Nothing. Look sis, I gotta run. I need to say my good-byes to the folks, and then I'm out."

"The folks?"

"The Carters."

"Oh," he really was part of the family. "Will I see you tomorrow?"

He glanced back across the room. "I don't think so. I want to check on something in Austin before we roll out. Love you."

"Love you more. Peak in on my place too."

"Done." He kissed her cheek and left. *What is going on with those two?*

"Babe, you ready to make our rounds?" Cameron kissed her and took Isaac's empty seat.

"As ready as I'll ever be."

They circled the room. He introduced her to Damian's parents, Bruce's parents, and finally they stopped at the Carters.

"Mom, Pops, I'd like for you to meet Sydney Jones."

He slipped a protective arm around her waist. "Sydney there are my parents Michelle and Curtis Carter."

"Lady Bird, it nice to finally meet you."

Sydney tensed, she hoped their meeting wouldn't become uncomfortable. Another odd revelation was none of the RSE team seemed to mention, nor mind her past. It was as if Cameron had scrubbed the incident from existence. No sideways glances, no questions, just gone.

"It's nice to meet you too sir."

"Call me Curtis baby." He kissed Sydney's hand.

"Pops!" Cameron groaned, Sydney struggled to not laugh at his obvious annoyance.

Curtis blinked an eye, and she swore he looked like Cameron with that eyebrow wiggle.

"Mom?" The whine in Cameron's voice made Sydney burst. She laughed until she cried as the two went at it.

"Baby, pay them no mind. He's crazy, and his children are too." A flash of humor crossed Mrs. Carter's face. "And Michelle is fine, dear."

"Thank you, Mrs. Michelle, it's great to put a face with a name. I've heard wonderful things about you both."

"My boys sure can pick'em." Curtis stepped closer, and Cameron shook his head.

"Go over there and flirt with your wife."

This was how their day went. The Carters were precisely who she thought and more. Sydney figured they had to be amazing based on their children. She also met the middle son Kyle and his sister Lauren.

They sampled food and listened to music while the kids played. The details for tomorrow's picnic were finalized, then they moved to another room to conduct the meeting.

They had the line up nailed down, and Bruce would send the files to the engineer later tonight. It was official. They had done it. The soundtrack was complete.

Celebratory wine flutes started flowing in, carried by waiters in formal attired.

"It's time for a toast." Sydney froze, Cameron kissed her temple. "Don't worry so much. We always have sparkling cider for Marques." She relaxed at his side and grabbed a glass.

"Ladies and gentlemen, bring it in." They gathered in front of Cameron and Sydney, feeling the extra eyes made her attempt to move aside. But his gridiron grip kept her in place.

"Really Cam?" She whispered for only his ears to hear.

"Damn right." He kissed her, then turned back to the team. "Glasses up."

Cameron started his speech, and a feeling of pride filled her. The day to day actions of going to the studio and working day in and day out had resulted in this moment. Cameron had led his team well. And each took their tasks and ran with it. She learned so much from them and looked forward to many more years to come.

"We are not done. This is truly just the beginning." He glanced down at her. "I'd like to shout out our new team members, Isaac and Sydney." The crowd clapped and cheered. "Let's toast to the RSE legacy, more music, more fans—

"And more money," Jamal shouted.

"And more money. To RSE…"

She touched her glass to his, and the others did the same. The men huddle in a group hug.

"Family…"

"Over fame!"

CHAPTER TWENTY

*T*hey managed to convert the RSE Headquarters into an amusement park. Cameron didn't want to know how much they spent to have a Ferris wheel and the petting zoo. He was certain Jamal had squeezed every penny and questioned every dime spent.

He arrived early to meet with security. The annual RSE picnic was a community affair that meant opening the security gates around the property. Bull and X were a security team out of Atlanta that handled the security for both locations and personal bodyguards for Marques and soon Sydney.

Cameron stepped out of his car and Bull walked towards him. His name was Wesley and towered over Cameron's six-foot-one-inch frame by several inches. Bull looked like a professional wrestler. Cameron feared for the person foolish enough to fall on the man's bad side.

"Are we set for today? Cameron leaned against his car.

"Yes, Mr. Carter." He sat next to him with X standing off to the side.

"You can expect the festivities will be concentrated in this area." Cameron motioned towards the oversized parking lot and open field. They planned to expand the compound soon once the entire team migrated to Houston.

"We took an extra precaution and have men patrolling the perimeters of the property since it's open to the public."

"Good." Cameron nodded. "Call me if you need me."

"Yes, sir."

Cameron left them to walk through the other areas. They had game booths, the food trucks, and the petting zoo for the public. Then a private tent for the RSE team. He rounded the corner of the building, and the wives were dashing from one end of the grounds to the other. He scanned the area looking for Sydney. He saw her over by the roasted corn truck.

He walked over and waited as she instructed him about the parking and loading areas.

"Hey, gorgeous." He kissed her cheek.

"Hey yourself."

"This is a massive event." The awe in her voice made him chuckle.

"I told you. We have a great time and build community awareness. It also serves as a back to school bash."

"I saw the school supply truck."

Cameron nodded. "Wait until you see the holiday party. Brione has a Single Mom's Suite."

"And Sandi?

"Her focus is community outreach for women with infertility issues. She turned it into a health festival. Last year we had all types of issues represented. I think you'd like that one too."

"Chop chop love*birds*." Eliana teased from behind him.

"Ha ha ha…" He watched her walk by pushing a helium tank. "I bet they give you a hard time."

"They do, and I love it. I never had sisters before, and I'm starting to see that was a good thing." They laughed and kissed their goodbyes. They both had work to do.

"I'll see you at the tent later," Cameron called out.

"I wouldn't miss it for the world."

SYDNEY COULDN'T RECALL WORKING SO HARD IN HER LIFE. From sun up to sun down people came and went. The music blared, and the food flowed with the constant screams from the Ferris wheel lingering in the background.

The RSE wives are the truth. Everything went without a hitch as the cleaning crew arrived. She checked with Jamal to confirm that the vendors were paid. He said yes, and she was officially relieved of her picnic duties.

The team would head over to the tent for soul food catered by The Daniels. But Sydney wanted to take a quick shower. It would take her about fifteen minutes to rinse the dirt off her skin and cool off. She thought about finding Cameron, but he'd turn a quick shower into a five-hour event.

Instead, she sent him a text.

I'm heading to use your private shower. I'll be back.

He quickly responded:

Okay. ::heart emoji::

She replied:

::heart emoji::

Sydney crossed the parking lot heading to the main building and heard, "Looking good Lady Bird." His tone was velvet yet edged with steel. Her eyes darted nervously back and forth.

She spun around and came face-to-face with her past. One Time.

"Don't worry we're alone. The black Hulk went that way." One Time point back towards the tent. "Long time no see."

She lifted her phone.

"How about you give me that?"

"What do you want?" She didn't pass her phone. She had to talk with him long enough for Bull to circle back around.

"I want my lady back." His eyes roamed over her figure making her feel like slime. And to think she once fell under his powers of persuasion.

"One Time stop playing games. If you want to talk with me come back during normal business hours." She turned to walk away, and he grabbed her arm snatching her back around.

"This ain't a game. You owe me. You left the tour, and I was sued for millions. And you still owe me an album." He stepped closer, the anger in his eyes, made her do the next best thing. She kneed him in the nuts and turned for the tent.

"Cameron...Bull...X..." she yelled running on wobbly legs when she felt a yank. In a lightning-fast motion, One Time pulled her back against his body. He pulled her head back by the length of her braid.

"Bitch don't you know I'd—"

"You'd what?" Cameron's voice was as cool and clear as ice water. Sydney felt relief on second and dread the next. The anger in his eyes caught her off guard.

One Time gripped her throat squeezing tighter and tighter, cutting off the air. "Cam..."

Cameron dove for them, One Time roughly pushed her to the ground. Sydney rolled on her side gasping for air, fighting the dark spots blurring her sight.

"Cameron, that's enough man. Cam!" Mr. Curtis called out.

Sydney turned over, holding her sore neck to see Cameron driving his fist into One Time's face. Damian and Bruce were trying to pull him off with no avail.

"Cam, baby don't." Sydney tried to get up, and Marques helped her.

"Cameron, Syd needs you," Marques called through the commotion. The wives pushing the kids back to the tent. The men trying to pull Cameron off One Time. Security arrived just as Cameron drove his foot into One Time's stomach.

"Get this muthafucka off my property," Cameron ordered security. "Syd, baby." He turned as if noticing her for the first time. He picked her up from the pavement, resting her throbbing head on his shoulder. She could feel his rage as if it were her own.

"This shit ain't over." One Time called out as Bull and X took him away.

"You come near her again, and I'll make you regret the day you laid eyes on her." His deadly threat sliced through the air.

Sydney covered his mouth with hers. "He's not worth it. Baby look at me. Cam…please." She begged, his eyes conveyed the fury in him. She kissed him again. "It's okay."

She glanced around, and the RSE men flanked their leader like a hedge of protection. Thankfully the kids were gone, and Mr. Curtis stood behind Cameron with a hand on his shoulder. A stab of guilt laid buried in her chest. This was all her fault.

CHAPTER TWENTY-ONE

*C*ameron felt it all day. Something was off. He walked the grounds, pacing like a caged lion. He'd hired security, he'd kept an eye on her from afar, and the one moment he turned his back, this happens.

"I'm sorry," she whispered.

He covered her mouth with his, he could feel her shaking still. "Let's get you to a doctor."

"No, go back to the tent. Make sure the kids are okay."

"Sydney." This conversation was over. "Guys walk with me. Dad, we'll be back."

"Y'all stay with him." Mr. Curtis said.

"Yes, sir," Marques called back.

Cameron carried her to his car and lowered her inside. He closed the door behind her and stepped away from the vehicle. Damian and Bruce stood in front leaving enough space to keep his eye on Sydney.

"Don't make me catch a case over this dude." He looked at Damian.

"I got you, bro. Let me press a few connects."

Cameron turned to Marques, "Call Isaac and let him know what's going on. I'm taking Sydney home." He dropped his head for a moment flexing his hands. "I'm sorry guys, I lost it. "

"I'd expect nothing less, you have to protect your woman," Bruce said.

Cameron nodded not trusting himself to talk. "Thanks, guys. I'll keep you posted."

"Family," Damian called out.

"Over fame." He hugged each of them before turning to the car.

"Now, Tyson, we need you to go put those weapons on ice. And we'll close out the picnic." Devin teased sending the guys into a fit of laughter.

Cameron didn't know what he'd do without his brothers. He'd left the tent planning to surprise Sydney in the shower for a little interlude only to hear her call out his name. The fear in her voice made the hairs on the back of his neck stand up like guiding devices. He rounded the corner as One Time wrapped his hand around her throat and all Cameron saw was red.

He climbed in the car. "How are you?"

"Shook up but I'm better. I really want to go inside to let them know I'm all right."

"No Syd." He turned over the engine. "The guys will let them know. And I'll text Marques and have him grab a plate for you."

"Don't try to distract me with food."

"I'll do anything to keep you safe. Now get some rest."

"Thank you." Her eyes sagged closed.

THE DOCTOR CAME AND CHECKED HER OUT. SYDNEY HAD A few scratches and a bruised neck, but the doctor assured them she'd be back to normal by the end of the week. Cameron watched her from the corner of his eye. That spoke of the physical wounds by not the mental ones.

"Talk to me, baby."

"Hold me." She wiggled over to his side of the bed, resting her head on his shoulder.

Cameron did as his lady requested. They stayed around the house for a few days until the bruises on her neck cleared and then he arranged for her to go into the studio.

"We got good news today." She glanced over from her notebook. "They studio executive loved the soundtrack."

"Congratulations." She smiled, but the light didn't reach her eyes. He felt like he was failing her all over again.

"Syd, baby I need you to talk to me. I can't help if I don't know what you need from me."

"I want you to meet with One Time."

He pulled back. She must have bumped her head. "And why would I do that."

"How am I going to shoot a video without knowing

about my contract? If he doesn't release me, it could put your entire project in jeopardy."

"I *wish* he would. The fact that we're arguing about this just shows how ridiculous this is. Let him throw his best shot. I'll bury him and his label in so much litigation, h'is children's children will fear the Carter name."

"I've already done enough," she whispered.

"What do you mean, you've already done enough? This dude pops up and tries to harm you, but it's your fault. Do you hear how that sounds?" His frustration with the situation was on ten.

"He came looking for me. He won't let that go, Cameron, I know him. How do you think it makes me feel to see you plummeting your fist into a man's face because of me?"

"It should make you feel protected. That I'm not about to let him place a hand on you and think it's okay. Granted, I don't want to hurt another person. But him coming for my family is nonnegotiable." He cut through the air with finality. Cameron got up, "I need some air."

CHAPTER TWENTY-TWO

*S*ydney heard the front door close and reached for her phone. For the past few days, she'd been thinking of a plan. There would be no beef if she just finished out her contract. Then they all could go on with their lives.

But not if Cameron had One Time arrested?

She scrolled through her contacts and texted.

We need to talk. Can we meet up?

She wondered if he'd answer.

When? I'm at Club Black VIP lounge.

Give me 20.

Sydney got dressed and put on a baseball cap and a scarf. The bruising on her neck was still visible. She stopped for a second and considered calling Cameron. But the thought of him and One Time crossing paths again had her seeing the heading. *Billionaire music executive, arrested in Houston, TX, for attempted murder. Thanks to his junkie girlfriend.*

She opened the door to find Isaac about to knock.

"What are you doing here?"

"Cam asked me to come talk some sense into you." He scanned her up and down. "Where are you going?"

"Club Black." She stepped onto the porch locking the door behind her.

"Bird, what are you about to do?"

"I'm about to give One Time what he wants." She walked outside realizing she couldn't use the driver. He'd call Cameron as soon as he dropped her off. She turned to Isaac. "Will you please take me?"

"Bird this is *not* a good idea. That dude tried to strangle you."

"What do you think he'll do next? I can't have him coming after Cameron or the RSE family over me. *I* did this. *I* have to fix it. Now, are you going to help me or not?" She didn't want to drag Isaac in it.

"Call Cameron, Sydney."

"No. I have ten minutes. Or do I need to call an Uber?"

SYDNEY ENTERED CLUB BLACK, AND IT WAS JUMPING. SHE asked for the VIP Lounge, and the hostess pointed down the hall. The women were swinging on poles, and the men were making it rain. She made a deal with Isaac that if she didn't return in ten minutes to call the police and then Cameron, and he agreed.

A warning voice in her head scream, "Go home Bird!"

Truth be told, she was scared out of her mind. She knew One Time wasn't above harming her, but she was tired of being scared and holding her breath for the moment he popped up. Now was her chance to put this behind her. She only hoped Cameron would forgive her.

She stopped outside the VIP Lounge having dodge gropy-hand losers. She took a deep breath and knocked.

CAMERON SAW ISAAC'S CAR THE MOMENT HE ENTERED THE parking lot. The security guard called when he saw them get in Isaac's car. Cameron called, and Isaac told him where they were heading, never once giving away that he was talking to Cameron.

Sydney got out the car and went inside. Cameron got out with Damian. They walked over an talked with Isaac.

"What is she doing?"

"Something about recording the final album to finish out her contract," Isaac said.

"We'll be back." Cameron turned to walk inside.

"Cam let me come with you. I tried to go in with her, and she's talking crazy. She thinks this will help."

"I need you to stay here and call the police in five minutes. Okay?" He saw the worry in Isaac's eyes. "I'll get her. You did the right thing kid." Cameron tapped the door and walked toward the club.

Club Black was a premier gentlemen's club. He asked to rent a VIP lounge, and the hostess didn't blink.

"This dude is on the line for millions, but he paid ten thousand dollars for a VIP room." Cameron shook his head. He had to get Sydney out. There were two rooms. The hostess assigned them room two. It was safe to assume she was in room one.

"Stand back," Cameron whispered to Damian pointing at the peephole. But Damian halted him with a hand then flagged down a waitress.

"Can you do me a favor?" Damian asked the waitress, pulling out a hundred dollar bill and she agreed without hesitation. "Knock on the door. And wait until he opens it."

The waitress did as instructed. The moment the door opened they pushed their way inside. Sydney was inside, her eyes boldly met his. The table between her and One Time had enough drugs to send someone to prison for distribution. Damian stood blocking the door.

"Sydney, let's go." Cameron ripped out the words impatiently.

"Cameron—"

"What are you doing in here? Do you know what would have to your career if someone took pictures of you in here with all these drugs?"

The thump of the DJ outside disguised the rhythm of his racing heart. What was he doing here? *Trying to save someone that doesn't want to be saved.*

"Syd, we're leaving in five seconds. You can stay or leave, but once I leave, I'm done." Cameron said with finality.

"Oh, ain't y'all sweet. Lady Bird you traded me in for this weak dude? He did put you back in the game but baby girl you can do better."

"Cameron," she reached for him, not to leave but to stay.

"I'm done with this shit. Damian let's go."

Cameron left with her calling his name. He had no business inside Club Black, risking the careers of every artist under his leadership.

"Want me to stay back?" Damian asked.

Cameron looked back towards the room, "Please. Call me if you need me. I can't stay here. This is too much."

"Cameron, things are not always what they seem," Damian said.

"You could be right, but right now. I don't care. It's her life to screw up." He said the words but his leaving her inside would kill him. He stopped in the parking lot, counting the cost. Torn between walking away and going back and dragging her out.

"Cam, let me explain."

He did put you back in the game…

He won't let that go, Cameron, I know him.

Turning it over in his mind. She'd said on more than one occasion how much she *knew* him. And the alarm bells went off in his head like a fire station. He turned around to face her, "You were *with* that dude?

"On and off for a few years. But its over and it has nothing to do with tonight."

"I'm out of here." He walked away then doubled back. "You know what Sydney you're no different than Gabrielle, she wanted my money, and you wanted a deal. Congratulations Syd! I guess your man is right, I just put you back in the game. You're welcome."

Sydney reached for his arm. "Cameron, you know that's not the truth. I'm here tonight to finally finish my contract and put this behind me. And behind *us* for good."

She stepped closer, "Baby, I need for you to trust me. I have a good plan." He looked away but didn't move. "I have enough material to complete an album. And then I'm done with Southern Sounds and One Time for good. Please, Cameron, help me do this."

"I'll help you under one condition, you must do exactly as I say or I'll walk."

"I agree." A smile crossed her face, and it broke his heart because he knew what he had to do.

"And Syd, this between us is over."

"What do you mean?" She cupped his face in her soft hands, and he wanted to kiss the pained look off he face. But she's gambling, and the price is too high.

Cameron stepped back. "I'll help you finish off this deal with Southern Sounds. I can't do this. I have an entire team following my leadership, and I can't jeopardize their careers. Good night Syd."

"Cameron you're overreacting. Let's talk about this."

"Did we talk about it before you decided to take this

meeting? In a strip club? Surrounded by drugs and a man that tried to strangle you in front of me? Tell me, Syd. Why didn't we talk about that one?"

"No, because I knew you'd try to stop me."

"And that's why I'm leaving. That sounds like some toxic behavior to me. I can't protect you from *you*."

"Cameron, I'm a grown woman, and you can't control me. I don't ask for, nor do I need your protection. What I need is for you to stand by me. Stand by me and love me."

He shoved his hands in his pockets to keep from touching her. "My decision stands. This is business. I'll meet with you both tomorrow at ten o'clock."

"*Just* business," she called out.

"No doubt."

CHAPTER TWENTY-THREE

*C*ameron assembled the team at seven o'clock in the boardroom. He sat at the head of the table wondering how he got here again. He couldn't sleep in his bed—their bed—alone. So, he arrived at the office and worked all night on putting together a deal to free Sydney from Southern Sounds and give her the option of singing again.

The men chatted amongst themselves as he settled in his chair. He gave them an overview of the situation then pointed them to the specifics of the deal he planned to offer between Sydney and Southern Sounds.

"In this revised contracts, she will complete her existing writing contract with RSE without renewal. And I'll represent Sydney while she renegotiates her contract for her final album with Southern Sounds, against my recommendation."

He paused and assessed each of their faces. "But it's a setup. The revised contract includes a Key Man clause.

This means if Diesel "One Time" Armstrong is dropped for any reason, she's free and clear."

Damian sat forward, "After talking with a few sources I learned Diesel Armstrong needs this deal with Sydney to keep *his* deal with WW Music."

Cameron dropped his gaze to his hands, "I'm asking you guys to help me. Mr. Armstrong doesn't know, that we have this information. And we're using it towards our advantage to get Sydney a better deal. He needs her, and we're striking while the iron is hot."

"A better deal to leave us?" Jamal asked.

"Yes," Cameron answered. Sydney couldn't stay with RSE. He couldn't imagine seeing her, hearing her, smelling her, yet not having her. It would kill him.

"How will you negotiate her a better deal if the current contract is valid?" Marques asked.

"I will propose a substitution contract. We'll oversee her entire project, including the expenses. Southern Sounds must agree to give Sydney full creative liberty, that she will not owe for production, and to absorb any past debt. Of course, any expenses incurred by RSE in executing this deal I'll pay personally."

"Why would you agree to this type of deal?" Devin asked.

"To give her a fresh start." Cameron looked around the room, "I call for a vote."

"I'll vote yes if you allow us to shoulder the expenses together," Bruce said.

"I can't let you guys—"

"Then my vote is no." Bruce didn't back down, meeting his eyes. The other men nodded in solidarity.

"Then you'll agree to vote yes, only if RSE covers the expenses to produce Sydney Jones' final album with Southern Sounds."

"I agree." And it was a unanimous decision.

"Man, I love you guys." Cameron felt overwhelmed. He wouldn't have Sydney, but she would have her first love, music without the cloud of a shady deal with Southern Sounds hanging over her.

"Family…" Marques said.

"Over fame."

SYDNEY COULDN'T SLEEP. SHE LEFT CLUB BLACK IN A DAZE. One Time agreed to meet her at RSE. She went through the catalog of music she'd created since working with RSE. She had over fifty tracks.

But the knowledge of this deal only made her life worse because now Cameron thought she used him. She dressed and headed over to RSE hoping to talk with Cameron before the meeting. She prayed he'd let her explain.

She went back to the conference room, and the full team was there. The guys stood up to greet her, but her eyes remain locked on Cameron. He gave a tight nod, then pulled out the chair beside him.

Sydney sat in the offered chair with the scent of his cologne swirling around her. "Cam."

He turned her way, and she saw nothing. No light. No sparkle.

"I'm sorry," she whispered as One Time entered the conference room. The men stood, and so did she.

"Please have a seat." Cameron offered to One Time and his attorney.

Sydney glanced around the table, and she was the only woman. And she sat at the head of the table like the queen beside her king. The great leader surrounded by his team. She looked over at Cameron, his strong profile looked chiseled in stone.

This isn't over.

Sydney walked away from her career before out of duress. But she wasn't the same woman. She would show Cameron and RSE that this is where she belonged. With that resolve planted in her heart, she took the offered contract, making sure to brush Cameron's hand. And she saw a spark. She may be down, but she's not out.

Cameron and Damian negotiate her contract with ease. His direct delivery and command of the room made her grip his knee under the table. He jumped giving her a *behave* eye. She pretended not to understand his look. After the fifth knee squeeze, Damian called for a fifteen-minute break to regroup.

One Time and his attorney left, as soon as the door closed Cameron turned to her. "I need you to behave."

"I'm trying." She shrugged it off, and he dropped his head with a discreet smile on his lips. "But I have an addendum."

"And what's that?" Damian asked.

"I want a full release of my songs on the soundtrack." She saw a little more light in Cameron's eyes.

They called the men in and finished the negotiations. In the end, she received a new contract with creative liberty, no debt, release for the soundtrack, and a fresh start. But she'd have to deliver a finished album.

They signed. Southern Sounds gave her thirty days to complete it. One Time wanted to take advantage of the movie and soundtrack release.

The men filed out leaving her alone with Cameron. "You're all squared away."

"Why'd you do it, Cameron?"

"Because everyone deserves a second chance. This is yours. Now, make it count." His smile was as intimate as a kiss.

"Don't give up on me."

"Never, but don't give up on you and don't settle." Cameron stood to leave, and she grabbed his hand.

"I love you Cameron, and I plan to show you that you're wrong about me." Sydney stood and walked out on shaky legs. She knew without a doubt she was ready to give herself completely to Cameron. Now to convince him she needed to call her RSE sisters. She needed them to stage an intervention. *Would they help her?* There was only one way to find out.

CHAPTER TWENTY-FOUR

Sydney left RSE and headed to Coffee Confessions to meet with the ladies after sending a group text message. She had a lot of explaining to do. First the picnic then last night at Club Black.

Sydney never really had girlfriends, but in a short time, these women felt like the real deal. Like she'd known them her entire life. She wanted their help. No, she needed their help. To ask, Sydney knew she had to tell them how she got here.

Sydney sat with Sandi, Imani, Brione, and Eliana—the wives plus one. They huddled around the table, and Sydney told them about moving to LA, connecting with One Time, her near death, and her decision not to sing. But her story turned from the better after meeting Cameron and signing with RSE.

Sydney told them about her renegotiated contract and wanting Cameron back. "I did not betray his trust. I know I should have told him about meeting with One Time, but

I could only see one way to get out of the contract and keep making music with RSE." She let out a deep breath. "I was tired of sitting around waiting for the moment One Time would strike."

"We've all made mistakes, but why should Cameron believe you weren't in cahoots with One Time?"

"He shouldn't. I know how it looks. I can only give him my word. I went to the club to get this behind me." Sydney brushed away a tear, gripping the coffee cup like a lifeline. "You don't know what it feels like to try to move forward while always looking over your shoulder for the one person capable of snatching away the little bit of joy and happiness you've found. I have happiness with RSE. And I plan to fight for it with or without your help. But I need you to make it happen."

She stared down, then back up at the women. "I give you all my word. *I love Cameron*. More than anyone in my life. And I know I hurt him. It wasn't intentional, but I did, and I'll have to ask his forgiveness."

"I'll help," Brione raised her hand. "I know that feeling of running from your past and finding hope with the RSE family. They helped me get my baby back. You got me and my organization skills." She leaned over and squeezed Sydney's hand.

"Me too." Imani said, "Damian and I believe you. It just all came out wrong. I'll help."

"Good because I need some dance moves." Sydney smiled feeling a little more hopeful.

"Count me in then." Imani smiled and gave Sydney a side hug.

"You know I'm down for a fairytale ending," Eliana said.

"Fairytale?" Sydney asked.

"Oh yes. Don't laugh I've dubbed the RSE men dragon slayers." They laughed until Sydney's side ached.

"I got one better," Brione held up her index finger, "I believe they had a pixy dust factory."

Eliana nodded her head in agreement. "We'd identified the colors and everything!"

Their laughter flowed through Sydney, and she was glad she called on them. She had three on board. "So, Sandi?"

They all look at Sandi. Sydney noticed the wives differed to Sandi the way the guys listened to Cameron. Sandi sat thinking, not rushed or pressured to respond.

"I'll help. But Cameron has a special place in my heart. Treat him right."

Sydney nodded. "Thank you all so much. I promise I won't let you down." She took a deep breath and pulled out her notebook. "This is what I have in mind. The stage."

"A stage?" Sandi asked.

"Girl don't underestimate the stage. That's how Marques got me." Brione said. "My man knows how to work it, and I'm a sucker for it every time."

"And it's how Damian got me too." Imani smile. Their questioning eyes made her continue, "He danced for me and my munchkins."

"Aaaaahhhhh…." They gushed in unison.

"Damian danced?" Sydney couldn't imagine it. He

was extremely handsome, but he seemed to lurk. Not scary, but odd.

"Yes, don't let the olive skin fool ya!" Imani wagged her finger.

They slapped high fives around the table.

"I'm only hoping the stage will give me another chance. It worked once, and it's where I shine."

The ladies nodded and began tossing around ideas for how to make it happen and how to get Cameron there to see it.

"I got it." Brione nearly yelled, she looked at Eliana. "A release party."

"That could work. The soundtrack releases at the end of the month." Eliana pulled out her phone checking the schedule. "We'd have four weeks to make it happen."

"We've done it before with less," Brione added.

Then the real work began. Brione pulled out her notebook, and the ladies strategized for the release party of the year.

"We'll work out the details, you two work on the show," Eliana assured her, as Brione and Sandi nodded.

"I hope you're ready," Imani warned, "because this could get ugly."

I LOVE YOU CAMERON, AND I PLAN TO SHOW YOU.

Cameron was miserable, and only work could help. He had to keep his mind on business to push out his constant thoughts over her.

Everywhere he turned in his house he saw her. Her perfume lingered from her pillow. Her clothes in his closet. And he didn't have the heart to ask her to pick them up. Asking her would mean they were officially over.

He had to get out of Houston. Cameron climbed the stairs into the plane. He needed to spend a few days with the team in Atlanta office. He could spend some time with his mom since his father was on tour. Then he'd hit the road to scout a few artist showcases.

Love sucks.

He ran a weary hand over his face and glanced out the window as the city of Houston got smaller, fading into the clouds. Only time would lessen this ache and knowing he had to prepare for the soundtrack publicly didn't help his resolve to stay away from Sydney Jones.

He couldn't trust himself around her. She made him lose control. And that wouldn't do.

No more ruby lips, shower escapades, or funny Face-Time calls.

He had a brand to build. A legacy to uphold. A team to lead.

The satisfaction of seeing her reestablish her career would have to be enough. Now, if only Cameron could convince his heart the way he convinced his team.

A few hours later he walked into his childhood home. "Ma."

"Cameron, I'm in the family room."

He found her on the couch with her reading glasses perched on the end of her nose. "You look so studious."

"I look blind. Oh age, I tell you." She smiled, and it warmed his heart.

"And you still look good." He laughed pulling her into his arms.

"Thank you, baby." She leaned back and looked into his eyes. "I'll put on the tea."

"For what?" He said to her retreating back.

"Go put your luggage away. Have you ate?"

"No, ma'am." He loosened his tie, glad to be home.

"I'll fix you something while you shower and change."

Cameron shook his head. Michelle Carter was one of a kind. He followed his mother's orders, climbing the stairs to his old bedroom. He'd stay with her until his father returned. He could maybe take her to the spa tomorrow.

An hour later, he was stuffed and enjoying his father's favorite chair. His mother snapped a picture. The old man never shared his royal throne.

"I'm sending it to him."

"Good! It will teach him it's okay to share." They laughed.

"How did things work out with Sydney?" She removed her glasses and put her paperwork aside.

"We negotiated a new deal for her. She started working on her album last week. I think you'd like it." He kept his tone level. Her steady gaze said her motherly X-ray was helping her develop a diagnosis. "Stop Ma! You're making me nervous."

"What?" She snuggled into the corner of the couch.

"That thing you do with your eyes. You know what we call it?"

"I don't care what you call it. I call it a mother's love or motherly intuition."

He cleared his throat, "Code for nosey."

She laughed, tossing her head back and he got a flash of Sydney. Her laughter had a way of making everything better. He dropped his head.

"Tell me, son."

"Nah, it's nothing. I'm just tired from traveling."

"Lies!"

"I need you to stop watching ratchet reality shows."

She laughed again and it made is heartache and happy at the same time.

"They are a guilty pleasure. I can only take a few minutes, so I have to make it count." She chuckled. "What is this really about?"

He put his plate on the end table. He sat forward, elbows to his knees like the thinking man, searching for the right words. *What was this about?*

"I have a hard time trusting people." He paused grasping for his truth "And it feels like the more business success I achieve, the harder it is separate the sheep from the wolves."

"Why is that?"

He shrugged.

"We paid a hefty penny to educate you." Her smile held a secretive hue, she was digging for something. "You can do better than that."

"It's my expectations." He glanced over at her, "I have

this weird scale in my head constantly balancing the expectations of others with my goals. It started, I don't know, probably around the fifth grade. Dad attended a talent show, and I immediately went from Cameron Carter to Curtis Carter's son. The scaled was tipped towards the public perception. But I failed them this time." He fell back drumming his knees with his thumbs. "I let my feelings get in the way."

"Your feeling for Sydney?"

"Yes. I knew she was different, not just her voice but the way she moves, the way she conveys love and pain and a realness. I fell for her so fast and hard I didn't know it until I fell flat on my ass." His eyes shot to hers, "Sorry."

"Potty mouth."

"Potty, Ma? I'm not two."

"Use your words boy." She laughed and slid to the end of the couch closest to him. "Cameron, being an effective leader doesn't mean being hard, unfeeling, unrelenting. It makes you no less effective when you show your vulnerability." She grabbed his hand, "Those men follow you because you have a heart as big as Texas. You just don't know it."

He let her words sink into his achy heart. He was disappointed by how he handled his anger towards One Time, and he feared the idea of Sydney going back to the toxic environment at Southern Sounds when she'd come so far.

"Ma, it's not that easy."

"Why not?"

He shook his head in disbelief.

"You think its the accolades. But I think it's your fairness and loyalty. Your willingness to love the person not just the art. And the proof is in your ability to glue together the oddest people and produce a masterpiece."

His mother turned his face toward hers. "That's you, Cameron. And I think that's why you take the knocks of life so hard. You can't seem to separate people's actions from your glue. So you try to control everyone and everything, making it about *you*.

"Trying to pick the perfect pieces for your mosaic, but baby art is messy. Just like life. But it is also beautiful *if* you let it."

He wasn't convinced. He didn't do messy well. He liked order and consistency.

"Do you love her?" He opened his mouth to respond, and she stopped him with a slight tug on his arm "Scratch that question," she stared at the ceiling as if gathering her thoughts. "I have a better question. Does she make you smile? Laugh until you cry? Make you get lost in time? Do you miss her when she's away? Do you ache to touch her? Does her goals and desires, hits and misses, feel as real as your own?"

He couldn't hold her knowing gaze any longer. Every answer was yes, yes, *YES*.

"That is what I have with your father. And if I know nothing, I know this. We all need a soft place to land. A place where there are no expectations, no perimeters, and endless room to be flawed, yet loved. Even you Cameron Carter."

CHAPTER TWENTY-FIVE

*S*ydney thought her first few months with RSE were torturous, but this was more grueling. Her relationship with Cameron dangled in the distance like a carrot, insight, but out of reach. Her hope hinged on satisfying the thirty-day requirement for this album *and* giving an amazing surprise performance at the release party in Atlanta.

After signing the contract Sydney met with Bruce, they identified twelve songs of the fifty she recorded. Then they went to work. She had to clean up the recording, rewrite sections, and get them up to Bruce's standards. So, her days were split between recording all night and dancing all day with Imani, the *drill sergeant*. And Imani was worse than Bruce, she had her training like a professional dancer—everything hurt, even her eyebrows.

That woman was trying to kill me.

Sydney had to cling to the hope that this wouldn't be in vain. Telling her heart, she'd have Cameron back again.

And her broken heart felt much worse than her tired vocal chords and sore body.

Imani's desire to lose the baby weight seemed to fuel their intense dance sessions. But it had also snatched Sydney's waist. She chuckled, that woman had a baby and snapped back like a celebrity.

Today Sydney arrived early for her session with Bruce. A little birdie told her Cameron was returning tomorrow for a meeting and her heart leaped with joy. She dressed in her usual comfortable attire but added a little perfume. He said how it drove him crazy before, she might as well use it to help her get her man back.

She went into the studio and dropped her bag in the control room. Then she walked the halls of RSE like a fool in love. She wanted him to smell her fragrance everywhere. After taking a couple turns around the building she back to the couch to wait for Bruce.

Three weeks of sing, dance, repeat had her exhausted. She sat back on the well-loved sofa, deciding to review her song revisions. The chime of her phone stopped her. Was it Cameron?

When Eliana told her Cameron returned to Atlanta, she'd almost given up hope. How could she convince him if he wasn't here? So she reprised her *Get Cameron Back* campaign adding daily text messages.

Nothing major. Just funny gifs, inspiration quotes, anything to feel connected to him. Anything to hopefully remind his heart that it once loved her.

For the first ten days, Sydney thought she had the wrong number. He didn't respond to a single message.

No typing bubbles, no emojis, *nothing*. Her schedule didn't afford sitting around waiting for a response. Instead, she kept moving, kept singing, kept dancing. Then one day he sent a smiley emoji. No words. But it was a sign that there was life on the other end.

Sydney pulled out her cellphone, and it wasn't Cameron, bummer, but Bruce. He was running late. She quickly responded, "Okay." She'd wait since they had seven days to satisfy her end of the contract and time was ticking.

She tossed her bag on the floor and stretched out reading through her lyrics. She opened her phone and scanned through pictures on her phone stopping at her favorite of Cameron. He was smiling with that twinkle of mischief in his eyes. She touched the screen. She missed him.

"Stop Bird." She turned off her phone.

Longing led to worry. Worry led to doubt. Sleep was a better use of her time. She closed her eyes, a power nap would refresh her for a night of recording.

CAMERON ENTERED RSE. THREE WEEKS OF TRAVELING nonstop had him ready to sleep in his own house, his own bed. But he got a text from Bruce asking him to stand in with his session tonight. Apparently, Sandi and the kids had all taken ill, and he was the nurse on call.

Cameron dropped his briefcase beside his desk and stopped. He turned his nose up and immediately smelled Sydney. He glanced over his shoulder, taking a deep

inhale. Yeah, it was her sweet smell. He fought his decision to leave her in Houston for three weeks. He was no
better today than he was then. He thought space would
make his ache for her reside, but post-production of the
soundtrack meant constantly hearing her voice. Hearing
her voice brought up images of her face. And quite
frankly, he missed the hell out of her.

Then her text messages started popping up. He shook
his head. That woman of his found a way to reach out
every day. One day it was a viral video with a cat playing
the piano, she asked, *Think we have room for him in my
budget*. Another day it was a cute little chubby faced baby
showing her adorable "mad face." There were quotes,
samples from her album and the occasional, *I love you,
Cameron*.

His mother's words made him realize Sydney was his
soft place. Thirty minutes with her felt like fuel to his
soul. He knew he was flawed, and yet she loved him. But
he owed her an apology.

Cameron entered the studio, and the objection of his
ongoing debate was softly snoring on the couch. Bruce
warned him that she'd been working nonstop to finish
her album. And judging by her soft snores, she's
exhausted. The old Cameron would have scooped her up
and took her home. This Cameron didn't know what he
wanted to do about his heart. Because she had it, all of it,
and he didn't know if he could be the man she needed.

He kneeled beside the couch. The urge to touch her
won as he lightly brushed over the parade of freckles
across her nose and cheeks.

"Hey Cam...," she whispered as her golden eyes opened.

Their eyes locked, neither moving. He could say what she expected or walk away. The *Sin*Sations rule number four came to mind: Don't mistake the mic for the man.

Had that been his wrong turn?

He met Lady Bird, and now he knew Sydney Jones. Or just the opposite, he got to know Sydney Jones and Lady Bird was only a small piece of the woman he loved.

"I'm sorry." He stood, and she sat up. "Don't leave. Please."

The silence lingered for longer than he could imagine. But he didn't leave.

"I've learned a lot about myself these past three weeks."

"Tell me about it." He said, honoring her attempt to build a bridge between them.

"I learned the importance of family."

That wasn't what he expected. "How so?"

"I screwed this whole situation up."

"I wouldn't say that."

"You wouldn't. But I can." She pulled her knees to her chest. "The only consistent person I've had in my life is Isaac. Our parents floated in and out of their addictions, then they died. Then I come here, and you guys are like aliens."

Cameron laughed, despite himself.

"No offense."

"None taken." They shared a smile.

"It's like this perfect family, and you drop in the

outlier. I'm loud, I'm dramatic, I'm would people like to call eccentric, to be nice." She chuckled. "But beneath the stage wigs, makeup, and this voice," she touched her throat, "is a woman fighting for a piece of happiness. And just when I thought I'd outrun my eccentric ways, my past shows up and tries to choke the joy out of me."

Cameron moved to the couch.

"I thought I was getting better. That I'd learn a thing or two from the Carter bunch, but I'm still figuring this thing out. I didn't run again, but I tried to fix it, and I hurt," tears welled in her eyes, "the people I'd come to love so much." She used her sleeve to wipe her eyes. "And just when I thought it could get no worse, the RSE aliens still loved me," she laughed, without a trace of humor.

"Yeah, we kind of got that bad." He smiled pulling her against him. *God, he missed this*.

"*Aliens*." They laughed. "But I realize meeting with One Time was my decision to make, however, I should have talked with you. Not as my boss, but as my man."

"Syd, it wasn't my best moment either. I blew up. I just wanted to protect you. And yes, it hurt like hell. But I hope you know it came from a good place. You'd made so much progress, and it seemed like you were going backward."

"Cameron I know." She turned to look into his eyes. "Your actions show where your heart is, and I could have handled it better too. We're human. And it won't be the last time we screw up. I can only aim to not make the same mistake twice. That's where this whole, Carter alien thing comes in." Her smile beamed.

"How so?"

"Loving you means communicating. So, although I want you back. I've decided to show you."

"Oh really." He wiggled his eyebrows just to hear her laugh.

"No, stop!." She covered his eyebrows with her hands, he kissed her wrists.

"Syd, I missed you."

"Really?"

He wiped the lone tear rolling down her cheek. "Really. Forgive me?"

"Forgiven."

His mouth covered hers, and his soul screamed, *Aaaaahhhhhhh.*

CHAPTER TWENTY-SIX

A week later they rode through Atlanta to the album release party. She remained at her brother Isaac's house as she and Cameron fell back into their usual groove. He was curious about her visiting Harmony daily, but she just brushed it off as, "hanging with Imani."

"Are you sure, you're okay with going to the club?"

"Yes, Cam." He nodded. Sydney managed to keep her performance a secret. Going to the club was the least of her cares. Brione was handling the setup. Sandi her clothing. Imani and an additional dancer would back her up, and Eliana helped them keep it a secret. Everyone knew except Cameron.

"How does it feel to have your album done?"

"It's surreal. I think it's my best work. And knowing it will end my contract with Southern Sounds makes it even better. Have you heard from them?

"No. But with the soundtrack releasing Tuesday, I'm

sure they'll reach out by the end of the week." He kissed the side of her neck. "Will you come home with me tonight?"

"Are you ready for that?" She asked him. They'd decided not to make love. But she was ready to jump his bones last week.

"I miss you woman. We," he lowered her hand to his throbbing member, "miss you. I thought I'd collect on a few of my birthday suit vouches."

Sydney's laughed until she cried. "You're messing up my makeup."

"I could care less about your makeup, well except your lips." His slow sensual smile made her panties moist.

"What about my lips?"

"When you wear that ruby red lipstick, my mind and body go wild!" He shivered against her.

"That's good to know." She kissed him, slipping him a little tongue.

"Is that a yes?"

"Damn right!"

THE DRIVER OPENED THE DOOR. CAMERON STEPPED ONTO THE red carpet. He nodded to acknowledge the press and cameras waiting outside the venue. The team surprised him a few days ago with details about this release party, and it already felt like a celebration with Sydney at his side.

He reached inside and helped her out. She opted for a

white sequin dress similar to the black one she wore the first night he saw her. The fabric pooled at her feet, she'd called it a mermaid dress. Her hair was styled in waves cascading down her back.

Sydney worked hard with a glam team to prepare for tonight when all he wanted was to redeem his voucher because she looked *hot!*

They posed for a few pictures. Then all the cameras turned at the next couple in line. Marques and Brione. The cameras went wild, and they used the break to escape.

They entered the club, and the room was buzzing with energy. Eliana swooped in within minutes. "Hey, boss! Do you have your speech ready?"

"Speech? I didn't know I had to give a speech."

"I must have forgotten to tell you. Here take these few notes. We'll have you up after we start. Just the normal, thank you for coming, thank you for supporting our music, give a shout out to the Man upstairs, the usual."

Sydney snickered beside him.

"Don't you dare encourage that craziness." He laughed, shaking his head at Eliana. "I'll think of a few words. Is everyone here?"

"Yes. I'll show you to your area." She glanced over at Sydney. "You good?"

There was a discreet nod. After Eliana left them, he asked, "What was that about?"

"What?" She took a drink of water, she looked nervous.

"We don't have to stay Sydney."

"Stop worrying so much. I'm good. Promise."

The music flooded and they slow danced a few times. It felt good to see his cousin and the producers from the movie. They all were ecstatic about the soundtrack, and he now held his lady in his arms. His heart close to his heart.

"I'm proud of you Sydney."

She leaned back looking into his eyes. "Thank you."

"You made all of this work. We have the soundtrack, your album turned in, and next you'll have the world at your feet."

"I don't need the world, as long as I have you."

He kissed her cheek to keep from messing up her makeup. "I love you—"

"We're ready for you." He stopped to see Eliana. "Right this way."

SYDNEY WAITED FOR CAMERON TO ROUND THE CORNER AND headed backstage. She slipped in the dressing room and found Brione inside.

"Dress quick. You got until the end of his speech. I pray he's long-winded."

Sydney laughed, as her dress fell in a pool of fabric at her feet.

"We will rotate with each number," Brione said zipping her up. "Here's Imani. See you later girl. Break a leg!"

"Thanks, sis!"

Brione dipped out, and Imani joined her. "Look at those legs girl!"

"I got them from Imani's boot camp." Her dress was a fitted mini dress with her thick, toned, legs out. She had a dancing number and needed to have some room to get down. "She stopped by the mirror and freshened up her makeup. And added her ruby red lipstick. Pass my wig."

Imani helped her add her big curly hair, pinning it into place.

"Let's do this."

They walked to the backstage area as Cameron finished his speech. "Last but not least, I want to thank Sydney Jones…." He cupped his hands over his eyes searching the crowd, "This light is blinding. Well, thank you for gifting us with your amazing voice. We appreciate having you all, and have a great night."

Her heart was racing with adrenaline and love. *Love you baby.*

The crowd clapped, and Cameron was ushered off the other side of the stage. Bruce walked on, and the curtains closed. The crew started working like little minions setting up the instruments.

"We have a special treat tonight."

Her stomach dropped to her feet. She took a deep breath, Imani squeezed her shoulder. They walked out on the stage. The stage Sydney used to only associate with bad memories, now made her think of her love for Cameron. She stepped to the microphone, putting in her earpieces. She gave Isaac a thumbs up.

"I want you to put her hands together for the one and only Sydney Jones."

CAMERON DID AN ABOUT-FACE. *DID HE JUST SAY, SYDNEY Jones?* He stumbled at hearing her rumbling groan. He pushed past the people in the way, clearing the side of the stage as the curtains opened.

A single light shone from above, as the lights dropped around the club. Curly hair blocked her face but not her ruby lips. She stood in the middle of the stage in a gold mini dress with the little Tina Turner looking shimmies. Cameron moved to the center of the audience, when he was flagged down by the guys. He nearly ran, he didn't want to miss a single move or note.

He lowered to the chair, and he noticed the background dancers. "Who knew about this?" He asked in a hushed whisper.

"I did." Rippled around him.

He turned, "All of y'all knew, and nobody said *nothing*. I need new partners," he mumbled to himself.

They started a steady rock. His eyes were glued on Sydney. "How many of y'all know that RSE can do nice and easy? But tonight, I thought I'd do it nice and rough."

Each rock and sway caught the light sending glittering sparkles around the stage. The audience yelled, and she laughed, sending ripples through his body.

"Cam baby, this one's for you."

She opened with a *Proud Mary*. And with a spin of her dress, the show kicked off.

For forty-five minutes he watched hypnotized by his woman commanding the stage. And not a single person was immune. She changed outfits, dancing, shook, and shimmied until he was tired.

The stage went dark, and the thunderous applause surrounded him.

"Sydney. Sydney. Sydney." They chanted. The guys hollered and whistled. Several patting him on the back and he was so proud of her.

"Thank you. Thank you all." Her deep breaths echoing through the microphone. "Can I sing one more song?" The stage lights revealed her sitting on a stool in the middle of the stage.

"Yeah!"

"Ain't y'all sweet. I moved to Texas, and now it's y'all to *everythang*!" They laughed as she patted the sweat from her face. "I need my brother on stage for this one, go ahead, take your seats." The audience followed her command and so did he, sitting on the edge of his chair.

"This is only my second show, and I didn't do it alone. I want to thank the band, my dancers," she motioned behind her as the audience clapped, "and you." She clapped for them.

"Make sure you go out and see *Love Squared* in the movie theaters starting next week. Download or stream the soundtrack right now." She pushed her bangs up, smiling like a true star. "Well, after I'm done."

They laughed again.

"But most of all I want to thank Rockstar Entertainment." The crowd clapped, "Y'all can do better than that. Clap like you mean it."

The audience stood and clapped turning inwards facing their table. Cameron felt the sting of tears and fought to hold back his emotions. A round of hugs passed between them, and the crowd ate it up.

"Thank you for giving this Kansas City girl a second chance. For loving me when I was unloveable, and for giving me a song to sing. I dedicate this to *you*."

Her eyes locked with Cameron and he almost lost it. The lights lowered and her spell took hold of them. Sydney sung an acoustic medley of *Ashes*, *Damaged* and *Let Love Win*. Not a dry eye was in sight, including Cameron. Before the song ended he cut through the audience, running backstage.

Cameron heard her loud and clear. Every word shot like an arrow through his heart. The final note soared through the air, and the curtain dropped. Sydney looked spent, and Cameron rushed forward to scoop her up. The crowd cheered and screamed.

"Marry me."

CHAPTER TWENTY-SEVEN

*C*ameron carried her to the dressing room closing the door with a kick.

"Lock it."

"Yes, ma'am."

He lowered her to a chair with her cradled to his heart. His lips brushed hers, and she whispered, "Marry me."

Cameron leaned back, "You will be my wife but after *I* ask *you*."

"Where's the fun in that?" He laughed trickling kisses down her salty neck.

"Sydney Jones whining will not work. But no worries baby because you're all mine."

"Well, hurry up." Her head fell back as he teased her budding nipple through her dress. "Just tell me the time and place because all I need is you."

CHAPTER TWENTY-EIGHT

Sydney placed her iPad on the table talking to Cameron while she dressed.

"How does it feel to be back in LA?"

She shrugged sitting in the chair, "It feels like a lifetime ago. I wish you were here."

"I do too. I need to see this artist then I'll fly out."

The movie studio had her booked for several TV appearances thanks to the chart-topping single *Let Love Win* and the impressive box office sales for the movie. And she had her first video shoot for the soundtrack at the end of the week. It was all moving so fast.

"Are you nervous?" He asked.

"No, singing is the easy part. I only worry if they dig too far back in my past. But Devin coached me on addressing my overdose."

"I'm proud of you Bird." She smiled. "I'll get there as soon as I can. Marques is scheduled for the night show with you tomorrow. The studio is providing security. So, hang in there. Just get through the next couple of days."

"What's in it for me?" She wiggled her eyebrows.

His face lit up, "How about an exotic vacation? Just the two of us."

"I'm down like four flat tires."

He shook his head laughing, "Consider it done. Now get going, call me when you're done. Love you."

"Love you too."

They bounced around crisscrossing the country. Him scouting new talent and her fulfilling interview and performance requests. She was officially back in the game, not as Lady Bird, but as Sydney Jones.

SYDNEY FINISHED HER INTERVIEW AND HEADED TO THE waiting car. She was officially done and ready for a vacation. She noticed a missed call from Cameron. *I'll call him back.*

She turned to her temporary bodyguard. "Let's blow this joint."

"Yes, Miss Jones," he smiled and took her bags.

They exited the soundstage from the back door as the guard reached for her door her phone rang and "Lady Bird can I have an autograph."

"Sure—" She froze. "One Time, what are doing here?" Her phone rung again.

He stepped forward, and the bodyguard blocked him.

One Time peered around the guard, his mouth thinning in displeasure, "Damn, it's like that."

"Look I gotta go." She turned to enter the car.

"Wait!" He held up a hand, "I want to apologize about the whole picnic incident. I just wanted to talk to you like we used to."

"Apology accepted. Take care." She lowered into the car and connected Cameron's call as a blast shot through the air. A startled yelp caused her to look back. "What the—"

The bodyguard tumbled back against the car door holding his chest. "One Time...what have you done?" She dropped to the ground trying to help him, screaming, "Somebody call an ambulance."

"Get up Sydney! Get. Up!"

She rose to her feet concerned about the guard.

"I wanted to talk with you. But you blew me off."

"I'm listening One Time." She spoke in a calming voice, "I just need to get him help. He's losing a lot of blood."

"I helped you. Now I need you to help me." He leveled the gun in her direction. She saw a crowd coming from inside the studio.

"You don't have to do this."

"Stop talking to me like I'm crazy bitch! I need you to sign this." He tossed papers in her direction. "Sign it!"

"Okay...okay. I'll sign but what is it?"

"A new contract."

CAMERON CALLED SYDNEY FOR THE FIFTH TIME, AND SHE

didn't answer. Damian got word that One Time was dropped from WW Music. And the news didn't sit right with him.

Cameron rescheduled his appointments and jumped on the plane headed to LA. He dialed for the sixth time. She connected, and relief flowed through his body.

"Hey baby, how'd it go?"

A blast carried through the line.

"What was that? Sydney, Syd…"

She wasn't responding. He pressed the phone to his ear. The voices were muffled.

"Hurry up," he called to his driver, "And call the police."

CHAPTER TWENTY-NINE

$\mathcal{T}$aking a deep, unsteady breath, she stepped forward, "One Time…Diesel, please let me call someone. He could die." She glanced down, and his shirt was covered in blood. She hoped talking to him would give the police time to get here. "And I'll sign whatever you want. You don't want this man to die. It will ruin your career," she couldn't control the tremor in her voice.

"Ruin my career? What career? You left me. I've lost my deal. My only choice is to start over. And I need *you* to do it." The rage in his eyes

"I'll do it. Just let me call the—"

"Say another word, and I'll end this shit."

Over his shoulder, she noticed a police officer. He motioned for her to keep quiet by placing his index finger over his lips.

"Get over here."

"I need a pen." She had to stall. Visions of his hand

around her neck caused a cold knot to form in her stomach.

"Get it!"

She turned inside of the limo and noticed her phone on, she whispered, "Cam, help me, please."

"I'M HERE," CAMERON WHISPERED, JUMPING OUT OF THE CAR before it stopped. The police had them surrounded. He'd never felt so helpless in all his life.

"Lower your weapon," the officers called out. One Time's stood between Sydney and the police officers.

"Drop your weapon."

Cameron prayed he'd comply inching closer to the scene. He saw Sydney take a step back frantically watching the officers and One Time.

Baby don't move. The fright or flight looked beamed in her eyes as she took another step back. Then a blast sounded.

Pop, pop.

Sydney's piercing scream shot through him. Cameron ran for her limousine, screaming her name. The police grabbed him pulling him back.

"Is she all right? Syd. Syd. Tell me, please. Is she alright?"

SYDNEY SAW THE DECISION IN HIS GLASSY EYES RIGHT BEFORE One Time turned and pulled the trigger. She slumped to the ground uncontrollable tears flowing from her eyes.

"Syd. *Syd*."

"Cam," she whispered pushing herself up.

"Ma'am stay right there." The officer called out.

She nodded, searching the crowd for his face. "Cam, where are you?"

"I'm here baby."

"Officer, he's my boyfriend."

"Let him through."

She stepped around the bodies and leaped into Cameron's arms. And the tears took over, her body shaking.

"Baby, are you okay?" He held her back, checking her for wounds.

"I'm okay. Just hold me, please."

CHAPTER THIRTY

*S*ydney was sound asleep. But Cameron couldn't take his eyes off her. He almost lost her.

She went to the police station and gave a police report. Both men were declared dead at the scene. And he knew without a single doubt he no longer cared about perceptions or what anyone had to say. He planned to love this woman for the rest of his life, if she'd have him.

Sydney rolled over, "Come to bed."

He climbed in beside her, pulling her close until her body was on top of his. "Syd…."

"Uh huh…" she snuggled closer.

"Marry me."

Her head popped up from his shoulder. "What?"

"Marry me. Right now. Tonight."

"How? Why? What?"

"Say, yes, Bird."

"Yes."

TWO HOURS LATER THEY ARRIVED IN LAS VEGAS. THEY checked in to a chairman's suite at the Bellagio. She wanted nothing more than to become Mrs. Cameron Carter. However, she didn't want him to feel obligated to marry her.

"Cameron, you don't have to do this."

He looked up putting on his jacket.

"Sydney, actually I do." He stood and walked over, "I've tried to plan my life down to the minute. I tried to control it all. And tonight I almost lost you. If you want to wait, I'll wait. But I don't want to wait. I want to make you my wife and start a family." He kissed her lips. "We can plan a big wedding or a reception in Houston, Kansas City, Atlanta, Paris. I'll leave that to you. But you said, name the time and the place. The time is now, the place is here."

"What about your family?"

"They're on the way." His face spread into a smile.

"What?"

"Is that a yes?" He led her towards the door. "They'll beat us there if we don't get out of here."

She shook her head, "Aliens."

"Damn right. Come on fellow alien, I mean soon to be Mrs. Carter."

CAMERON STOOD BEFORE THEIR FAMILY AND FRIENDS AS Sydney walked down the aisle in a mermaid dress with a long train. Isaac walked her down the aisle. They decided not to have an official wedding party. Instead, they all would serve as witnesses.

They stepped forward, turning to each other. Cameron lifted her veil and brushed the tears from her eyes.

"Bird, your tears are killing me." He held her to his heart, whispering in her ear, "We can wait."

She shook her head feverishly, "Not on your life."

He chuckled kissing her upturned face. "The man is waiting."

They both glanced over at the officiant, and the wedding began.

"Sydney and Cameron decided to write their own vows. Cameron."

"I, Cameron Carter take Sydney Jones to be my wife, in front of God and our witnesses. Sydney, I promise to love, honor, cherish, and remain faithful to you." He paused looking over at the audience. "I know this isn't conventional but can I just talk to you baby?"

"Yes." She squeezed he hands stepping closer.

"I never thought I'd get married. I thought I'd remain a bachelor."

"Playboy Carter," she whispered.

"Yeah, Playboy Carter, but from the moment I met you, I knew you were different. I thought it was the music. But baby it's your heart." He touched her chest.

"I fought it. And then my mother asked me some questions, and I'd like to answer them today." He glanced at his mother, as she wiped the tears from her eyes.

"I love you because you make me smile, you make me laugh until I cry, you make me get lost in time. I miss you whenever you're away. I ache for your touch, and to be touched by you. I feel your goals and desire, hits and misses as if they are my own.

"Will you grow old with me?" She nodded, drying the tears from his face.

"I love you Sydney with every part of my being, what's mine is yours, forever and always. From this day forward until death do us part."

"Sydney."

"I, Sydney Jones take Cameron Carter to be my husband, in front of God and our witnesses. Cameron, I promise to love, honor, cherish and remain faithful to you. And I'll gladly submit to you. I love you and I'm so thankful you've taught my heart how to love again." Her voice cracked.

"You taught me the meaning of family, friendship, companionship, and loyalty because it is who you are. Thank you for believing in me and loving me even when you didn't know if you could trust me.

"Cameron, I'll never give up on you or our love. I pray that when we fall short, our love will pick us up.

"You're my light. My heart. My everything. I look forward to building a life and a future with you.

"I am blessed and eternally grateful for the honor of calling you, my husband.

"I love you Cameron with every part of my being, what's mine is yours, forever and always. From this day forward until death do us part."

They exchanged rings.

"It is with this in mind that I pronounce you husband

and wife. Those who God have joined let no man put asunder. You may now kiss your bride.

He lowered brushing his lips across hers, "Hello Mrs. Carter."

"Hello back."

She grabbed his face, and he held her close kissing Sydney until her love simmered down into the depths of his soul.

"I present to you, Mr. and Mrs. Cameron Carter.

"Gentlemen, let's get this meeting going. Y'all don't want Sydney Carter storming in and dragging me out."

"Sign me up for that show," Devin called out.

Jamal laughed at Devin's antics as the others settled around the conference table. He turned the top on his bottled water, convinced someone had drugged the Houston water supply. In less than five years, Bruce, Damian, and Cameron had married.

Jamal silently shook his head. *Not him.* Unlike the others, his family did not carry a celebrity name. His path had been his grades and an Ivy League education.

"Time is money fellas." He reminded them glancing at his watch. He had a flight back to Atlanta.

"Midas has spoken," Cameron said from the head of the table. The men chuckled but turned to start the meeting. "I have three matters of business on the table before I leave the country. First, we officially inked the deal with

Sydney for her first album with RSE." The guys clapped. "To ensure we have a proper kickoff I want to hold off on releasing her project. I want some time to sit with you all and plan a proper release. So, kick that around in her heads while we're away."

"Will we release the album she planned to submit to Southern Sounds?" Jamal asked.

"Yes, I'm sure Bruce may make a few adjustments, but they'll be minimal."

Jamal nodded. That would keep the label from over-spending on the project. He made a note to recheck the figures and meet with Bruce before Cameron returned.

"Second, we need to find a better model for scouting new artists. I want to limit my travel, but I don't want it to affect the quality of the artists."

"Have you thought about YouTube?" Marques asked.

"That's cliche." Cameron tossed back.

"What about a contest? Music reality shows are popular and easy to promote." Devin suggested.

"We could run a contest using YouTube submissions," Jamal said merging the two ideas. "It would save money and probably give you more submissions than you can handle."

Everything Jamal learned about the music industry came from the men in this room. He'd turned his millions over several times. They held investments in several, but the thought of launching a label hosted contest would increase the public appeal for Rockstar Entertainment.

"I like the sound of that." Cameron leaned back. "Let

me think about it. Jamal, can you work up some numbers for me?

"Certainly."

"Second order of business I need someone to swing over to New Orleans and meet with Carmela Franklin. He tossed the file on the table."

"Why her?" Bruce asked, flipping through the file passing it down the table.

"She is a hip hop artist that managed to fan-fund over half a million dollars to produce an independent album."

"Half a million? Why would she want to sign with us if she has the money and the fan base?" Jamal asked reaching for the folder. He raised his eyebrows, not what he expected.

"That is for her to explain because she reached out to us after hearing about us signing Sydney. Do we need to draw straws gentlemen?"

Her black crop top revealed her chiseled six-pack. The picture had her posing in front of a colorful graffiti wall. But Jamal's eyes went straight to hers.

"I'll go." Jamal's quick response caused all eyes to turn his direction. "I need to get out of Houston. The water is contaminated with *marriage* bacteria." He chuckled, but the woman staring at him made his joke not so funny.

"Midas it is. Keep the folder. Gentlemen, our king, and queen have been installed. It's time to kick this baby into overdrive. It's time to strike while we have a heavy buzz about RSE." Cameron made eye contract with each man at the table. "It's almost a new year, so be prepared to hit the ground running. The goal is to double our roster. I'm off to honeymoon with my bride. Make sure the building is in one piece when I return."

They laughed and hugged, bidding Cameron farewell.

The conference room cleared as the men parted ways, Jamal remained. He opened the folder again lifting the picture intrigued by his response to her. Carmela's long locs cascaded over her shoulder, her eyes peering straight at him. The chaotic wall paled in comparison to the strong posture of her stance.

Jamal had no desire to boo up any woman. His goal was simple, make it to a billionaire dollars. He planned to show all those foster homes that passed him up and the parents who gave him up that he was a self-made man. He had no time for a boo. But a sample of Carmela had a ring to it.

A little gumbo and étouffée with a side of Carmela held an enticing appeal. Jamal snatched up the folder, *New Orleans here I come*.

DEAR READER

Dear Rockstar Romance Reader,

I find writing this short letter difficult. lol So, I'll speak from my heart.

Thank you for reading ROCKSTAR SINNERS!

Why sinners? Well, we all fall short. And writing this story took me on a journey as I explored the rough edges of Cameron and Sydney's struggle to choose a healthier life, both had to choose to be a new version of themselves.

I hope you enjoyed it.

I also decided to include a little "chart" type page next for the "Men of RSE." Get caught up with the guys while I work on Book 3, ROCKSTAR BILLIONAIRE.

And don't forget to please leave a review. Thanks again.

Take care and *happy reading*.

Ja'Nese Dixon

www.janesedixon.com

THE MEN OF RSE

You can find the men of RSE in other books.

CAMERON CARTER

- *Rockstar Sinners*

ANDREW "MARQUES" CARTER

- *Rockstar Secrets*

BRUCE DANIELS

- *Caramel Surprise*

- *Love's Hope*
- *Hidden Desire*

THE SMITH FAMILY

- Yuki and Dylan … *Yuki's Luck*
- Jazz and Asher … *Asher's Sonnet*
- Rhonda and Jaxon … *Smith Surprise*

Did you enjoy *As You Wish*? If so, will you join my newsletter? You have two main options:

- Weekly: Giveaways, exclusive reads, updates.

- New Releases Only: This is about every 4 - 6 weeks or so.

You can unsubscribe anytime. But joining means you'll get updates directly. And hopefully, I'll "see" you again. Soon.

For more information visit http://www.janesedixcn.com.

Millions of adoring fans dream of having one night with him, but only she has access to his heart.

Born with three commas in his bank account and melodies in his veins, Marques Carter is the rising prince of R&B. But not even his family name can guarantees success.

Brione Allen is a smart woman that made a dumb decision: trusting the wrong man. He blackmailed her family and now she's bound by a debt they knew she couldn't pay.

A chance meeting leads to an encrypted proposal: One week, one hundred thousand dollars, one incriminating secret. But when extortion and family ties expose them to the worst of the limelight, which secrets will they keep...and which will threaten their small light of hope?

**Get Your Copy on Amazon
or Read in Kindle Unlimited!**

*My love is
yours to have.*

ROCKSTAR

Billionaire

JA'NESE DIXON

Get Click HERE to get the
Alert for Rockstar Billionaire.

He's stolen her heart, it'll take luck to get it back.

Just her luck, one evening after too many shots, Yuki wakes naked tangled in Dylan's expensive sheets. Yuki Smith doubts her mother's judgment on men, life, and definitely on naming her "lucky."

Dylan Jameson is her twin's best friend and all the things she's not. Filthy rich, focused, and drop-dead gorgeous. And beneath it all he is a really great guy. Then he messed it all up by asking for what she could not give, commitment.

Dylan heads to Ireland, somehow he took her *luck* with him. Now Yuki must board a plane to god-knows-where, to encounter god-knows-what, hoping for a chance to tell Dylan the truth. Because he's captured her heart and something tells Yuki she'll need *luck* to get him back.

Get Your Copy on Amazon
or Read in Kindle Unlimited!

CHAPTER ONE

"*P*ut up your mugs."

I reach for the heavy crystal tankard mug, extending it across the table towards my twin brother, Asher Smith, careful not to let my eyes slide to his left. He sent a cryptic text message.

It's on!!! Meet me at the spot in an hour.

I finalized the email I was typing, told my assistant to forward my calls to my cellphone, and now here I am in a bar at three pm with Asher, his wife Jazz, short for Jasmine, and his best friend and business partner Dylan Jameson—the one I'm avoiding in public. It's complicated.

"What are we celebrating? And hurry cause I'm hungry." I ask as my heart warms, pride does not start to explain the feelings tumbling in my chest. The smile on his face tells me it's good, really good. But I use this moment to give him a hard time. I mean, isn't that what sisters are for?

"Patience is a virtue." Asher says over his glass.

"Bite me, kid brother." I kick him. *That'll wipe that smug look off his face.*

"Ouch! And you're wearing those god-awful pointy heels." The gang laughs. I lift my legs to avoid the sweeping motion of his foot as he tries to return my sisterly love tap.

"Children, children," Dylan chimes in, "stop teasing. Get to it. I have plans." And I break my rule as my eyes meet his. Always the mediator. His strawberry blond hair, piercing blue eyes, and his wicked smile. He winks, and my heart skips a beat. Everything about him reads off limits. But like a child fascinated by the fire, I reach for the flames praying I don't get burned. Not my smartest move.

The waiter returns with our standard order of spicy wings, seasoned fries, and Dylan's insisted upon house salad on the table. And we're still waiting on the reason for this gathering in the middle of the day.

Jazz sits her mug down places her elbows on the table turning towards Dylan. "It must be a woman. For you to pass on wings and beer—"

"And the salad—" He adds.

"We all know ain't nobody touching that tired salad but you. Who goes to a sports bar for salad?" Asher looks throughly confused.

"Asher, focus." I cut through their banter. "What happened to the toast? Y'all are the worst." I reach for a wing and Jazz, my hopeless romantic sister-in-law, smacks my hand and the slippery chicken tumbles to the table. "Ouch."

"That's for kicking my husband." She winks and has the nerve to laugh.

"Thanks, babe." Asher leans over the table and kisses her dismissing the raised mugs in the air, our food getting cold, and the ticking clock.

"Get a room. Make the toast already cause this mug is heavy." I retrieve my wing praying the five-second rule applies. Dylan drops his head chuckling.

"Okay, okay. We closed on a space for Smith & Jameson."

"What?" I spring to my feet, and my wing flies across the room. "Sorry," I say to no one in particular as I round the table, pulling Asher into a hug. "I knew it. I knew you would get it."

Asher and Dylan were finding it difficult to secure a location for their international beer garden and eatery. They wanted a space near downtown but roomy enough for at least six truck vendors to park and offer food. But finding adequate space stalled their brilliant plan.

"Your call did it." Asher said.

I pull back placing my hands on his cheeks. "No, your business plan did it. I'm just doing my part."

"My good luck charm." He whispers under his breath for only us to hear. I hate when he calls me that, and he knows it. "Don't give me that look." He holds up a finger. "Let me have this moment. Please."

"Okay." I reluctantly agree.

"Thank you." He kisses my cheek, the joy dancing in

his eyes is infectious. I feel a silly grin matching his spread across my face.

"You're welcome." I go back to my seat, we lift our mugs with more vigor this time.

From struggling to this. I'm Vice President at Brand-Share and up for a major promotion to partner. He's independently wealthy from his business ventures, and he's on course to build a legacy with the Smith name on it. I look over at Asher, certain it will only get better.

"In the words of William Shakespeare, 'It is not in the stars to hold our destiny but in ourselves'. My destiny is connected to each of you and I'm a blessed man." He smiles at Jazz as she brushes away a tear. "This toast is to my beautiful wife, talented and uber-wealthy best friend, and my *twin*."

"And Momma," I add. "Don't forget Momma."

"Never." Asher's head drops for a brief second and when he looks up again, his eyes are glistening with unshed tears. "I will not fail with odds stacked so perfectly in my favor. We have a prime location in downtown Austin, the vendors, forty-nine of the fifty craft breweries on board, and in three days we're off to Ireland to secure a deal with one final brewery."

Dylan places a hand on Asher's shoulder. "Man we got this."

He nods. "Let's toast to Smith & Jameson Beer Garden. That we get the final contract with Impose Brew and we open our doors to the public by the summer. To Smith & Jameson."

We repeat as our mugs chime reflecting the excitement

swirling around our table. I tap Asher's glass. Then Jazz. Then Dylan, and our eyes hold longer than they should. I'm frozen. The sounds in the bar and of Asher and Jazz talking cease to exist. He mouths, *Don't be late*. I look back and forth to ensure no one saw it but me. He smiles and I find the strength to pull from his vortex.

We pass the time drinking beer, eating wings, and Dylan steps away to take a call and Jazz heads to the ladies room.

"When will BrandShare make their partnership decision?" Asher asks.

"Soon. They usually announce it by now, I don't know what the hold up is." I lick the spicy sauce from my fingers. I push around the contents on the messy table searching for the little wet towelettes. "I inked a deal for $5 million dollars yesterday. I'm just hoping that's enough."

"That should guarantee your offer." He finishes off the fries passing me a napkin.

"I hope so."

BrandShare is a boutique marketing firm I joined after graduate school. My department specializes in subscription boxes. I pair companies with products as a means of expanding their presence in the marketplace and increasing brand recognition. My clients range from high-end cosmetic companies to custom chocolatiers. I'm on track to making partner by my twenty-seventh birthday less than two weeks away.

Waiting for them to announce it is killing me. Then it hits me. "What if—"

"Don't worry. They're slow, not stupid."

"Brother you are totally biased." I smile appreciating his unwavering confidence in me.

"Damn right. Join Smith & Jameson, we can use that marketing brain of yours." He leans forward, I shake my head. That's not an option.

"One Smith is more than enough to secure the legacy. Besides, I have a job." I try to sound nonchalant about it. Sure it has become more of a grind than a passion, becoming a partner would give me more control of the clients I work with and inject some excitement back into my career.

"It's not only about *our* legacy. This is our family business." His knowing eyes scan my face, and I glance away. "Is that the only reason you won't accept my offer?"

The beer garden is their business. And the rest of his statements sounds like the Charlie Brown teacher in my head as I see *him*.

"You two think y'all have us fooled." I hear through the haze. "We all know you guys are attracted to each other." He motions across the room towards Dylan talking with another woman. "Just get together already and save us the awkward tension."

"There's no *together* for me. And *what* tension?" I roll my eyes, over this conversation. "BrandShare, you, Momma, that's more than enough for me."

"Being alone sucks." Asher states.

"I'm not alone I have you."

"Big sis, I pray you find a man truly worthy of how

precious you are." His eyes pierce through my facade and hit his intended target—my fragile heart.

"Yeah right. I'm the ball buster, remember?" I laugh. His grimace says he's not buying it. "My hands are full. Partnership. Your spot. And who knows I may finally take up a hobby."

I look over again, Dylan is retrieving his phone from the gorgeous petite blonde. He drops it in his pocket. *Player*. I need to get out of here. I find the wet wipes and clean the remaining sauce off my hands as Jazz returns, her face tense. I turn a questioning gaze to Asher, his face clearly reads, *Don't ask*.

"I'm out. I want to stop by my office before heading home." I toss the dirty wipe on my plate grabbing my purse from the back of my chair. "Congratulations again."

"Babe, I'll be back." Asher stands as I do.

"Stay here. I'm fine." I motion for him to sit back in his eat. "My car's right across the street."

"I'm walking Yuki to her car." He talks over me, kissing Jazz's check. Then he places a hand on my lower back guiding me to the front door.

"Good night Jazz," I call over my shoulder. "See you Sunday." *Call me*, I mouth. She nods, I send her air kisses. "Love you."

The sports bar is near capacity. Which isn't a surprise since they have Friday night half-off Happy Hour. I maneuver around people, tables, and chairs, finally reaching the exit. "What's that all about?"

"We're in a rough patch. I hope getting this trip behind us will relieve some of the stress and get us back to honeymooning." He opens the door, and I step out into the chilly evening.

"Is there anything I can do?"

"Nah, you've done more than enough. I predict…." Stopping next to my car, I turn with a smile. We've played this game since we were kids and now my very grown, very handsome brother is once again predicting our future.

"Oh, brother." I roll my eyes. "You do recall that you get it wrong about one hundred percent of the time. I appreciate your tenacity." I pinch his cheeks.

"Such a hater." He flicks his hand in my direction like he's shooing a fly away. He chuckles shoving his hand in his pockets, then he pulls me against him. Together we lean against my car as if our destiny is written in the Austin skyline.

"Did you ever think we'd be here?" He asks so low I almost miss it.

"Like physically? Against my car, in a parking lot?" The sun is dropping, and the breeze is perfect.

"Are you charging for these terrible jokes? Because you are laying it on heavy tonight." I dig my elbow into his side. He folds over laughing. "No, smarty pants, our lives."

"Never. Do you think it will get better?" I rest my head against his shoulder, his head now resting on top of mine.

"I know it will."

"Then tell me, oh wise one. What do you predict?" I trust very few people in my life, and this man is one of them. If he says the sky will be purple in the morning, I will bank on it. Only one other man comes close, *Dylan*.

The sound of chatter rings through the air as if the bar door was opened and closed. I glance toward the door, and there's Dylan. He taps the face of his watch and disappears.

I wonder if Asher noticed but he continues, "This time, two weeks from today, our lives will change for the better. You will be 27. You will be the first female partner at BrandShare. Smith & Jameson will secure the contract with Impose Brew and my marriage…" his voice drops.

"Will resume the honeymoon," I finish for him, placing my hand on his chest. I kiss his cheek, disarming my car doors. "It'll work out, you'll see."

He glances down into my eyes, and a faint smile crosses his face. I squeeze his arm and lower inside my car. "When are you telling Momma?"

"Let's do it in the morning. Meet me over there. We'll go to breakfast."

"Cool. I'll be there around nine. Love you."

I sit in my car staring at Asher's retreating back. Images of Dylan chatting with that petite blonde hanging on to his every word. What am I doing? Comparing myself to the blonde?

No.

Maybe.

Flipping down my visor, I touch up my lipstick, and my mother's face stares back. I slap it closed and try to scrub my thoughts clear of any comparisons to her. I pull the visor open again.

"Yuki, you control your destiny. You are a partner. No more secret meetings with Dylan. No more comparing yourself to petite blondes. No more Dylan." *I said that already*. I close the visor and rest my head on the steering wheel. It can't hurt to say it a few more times. "No more Dylan, no more Dylan, no more Dylan."

"*D*o you have a reservation?" A man in a penguin suit asks from behind a podium. I glance over his shoulder, and the inside is formal with white linen and soft candles. It echoes one sentiment, romantic.

No more Dylan. No more Dylan. No more Dylan. This chant isn't working as images of his smile, his eyes and a low rate hum ensue. The one I get every time I think about him. Every time I see him. It happens more frequently. This romantic dinner will not help.

Before Asher married Jazz the three of us did everything together. Then our three became two. It felt odd without Asher at first. Over the past year, it became something we did. Every Saturday. Movies. Museums. Concerts.

Missing our third wheel this time alone feels intimate. And although our secret meetings aren't really a secret we have never had a candlelight dinner. But this is the address he sent by text this morning.

"Ma'am." His annoyed glare bores into me.

"Ah, Jameson, Dylan Jameson." He scans the list under a reading lamp, my stomach's in knots.

"Dylan, what are you doing?" I whisper searching the room for his familiar face.

"I want to celebrate your birthday." His silky voice holds a challenge. I stumble back connecting with his chest.

"We shouldn't." Dylan steps closer planting his large hands on my hips.

"Of course we should."

"Sir." The suit insists.

"Give us a second." Dylan turns me to face him as he scans my body from head to toe. A singe of heat accompanies his roaming appraisal of my black dress paired with silver heels. "Yuki. Join me. Or I could celebrate your birthday alone." I see his smile before his head falls.

"How do you plan to celebrate my birthday without me?" I punch him in the arm. "You don't have to do this." I glance again over his broad shoulders at the impatient suit.

"I know how important twenty-seven is to you."

I don't buy *luck*. However, on my seventh birthday, Momma adopted me. I graduated college at seventeen. Twenty-seven looks as promising as the others. This is the downside of knowing him for most of my life. There are very few secrets between us. I stare up into his blue eyes, and I shiver.

"We *could* dine upstairs," he offers.

Taking a deep breath. Upstairs means fewer eyes, we would be alone. Alone, *alone*. But this is Dylan, we've spent time alone before. I roll my shoulders back and close the space between us.

"What's upstairs?"

"My penthouse suite." His smoldering eyes are melting my resolve to treat him like a brother. Hell, I've known him since we were seven. Nothing about this man mirrors his seven-year-old self except maybe the honesty hidden in the depths of his eyes. And memories, really great memories.

The suit clears his throat a few times, and Dylan glances back with a raised brow. And the suit nervously walks away to seat a couple.

"What do you say?" Dylan asks.

As a marketer and a saleswoman, I close deals. It is what I do. I tell colorful tales, full of hope and potential fused with a dedicated focus. I am a visionary. I see the unseen. I get paid millions to do it. But this is hard to envision. I can't see how this will end.

How can our friendship remain intact? How will Asher feel if it all blows up in our faces? If Dylan learns….

"Dinner. Drinks." He restates casting his own vision for tonight.

"*Just* dinner and drinks."

"Baby girl, we passed just dinner and drinks a long time ago. I want more. Much more. You know it. I know."

He pauses letting his words penetrate my apprehension. "But I'll accept what you offer."

I bite the inside of my lip counting the cost. "So dinner, drinks, and—"

"You in my bed beneath me."

The air swooshes from my lungs. His intense gaze melting through my objections. And then his mouth covers mine. In front of the suit, the other waiting patrons. Soft and persuasive. His large hands grip my waist pulling my body to his. Intense, yet familiar.

Our first kiss.

He pulls back. "Yes?"

I swallow, my body swims with desire at seeing this Dylan for the first time. "Yes."

Dylan grabs my hand as if we've done it a million times before guiding me through the lobby with nonchalant grace. *Am I really going to his place?*

He stops in front of the elevator and presses the up arrow. I use the time to catch my breath and return his assessing gaze. His polished shoes and suit are expensive. The soft sheen of the navy blue fabric against his olive skin paired with a crisp white shirt and a power red tie. He screams wealth. But its the full beard trimmed low that imparts the right amount of edge to his pristine appearance.

I'm glad I picked my best black dress. The knit fabric hugs my curves with a plunging v in the front, the back is open with double straps. It's what I call sexy in the front, vixen in the back. I straightened my bra strap length hair and adorned a smokey dark eyeshadow look with ruby red lipstick.

"Yuki you look gorgeous tonight." He leans against the wall, powerful with his arms crossed over his massive chest.

Ding.

The elevator doors open and his hand finds my lower back. A hiss escapes under his breath. I glance over my shoulder meeting his gaze. Dylan is taller than my brother by at least two inches. I feel like a smaller woman in their presence, which is rare for my five-foot eleven-inch height.

"Where's the rest of your dress, Miss Smith?" His eyes dance with mischief.

"Do you not approve Mr. Jameson?" The ease of our normal banter settles between us as the elevator doors close. I spin around to face him. The sparks in his eyes thrill me while my attraction for him bubbles to the surface terrifying me. Feelings I've run from my entire life.

Love is not in for me. I am the evidence of love going terribly wrong. My veins hold conflicting truths fusing my parents and severing me from my living relatives residing in Korea. My black father and Korean mother banked on love and lost.

He presses the PH button and enters a code on the keypad. The doors close. We are alone. He takes two giant steps, his eyes zero in on my silver body necklace. His index finger runs the length from my neck, down my chest, between my breasts. I inhale his familiar scent.

"Why is this the first time you've invited me to your place?" I ask.

"I had to wait for the right time."

"For what?"

"For you to hear me out." His voice low and smooth speaks volumes as his large hand brushes my exposed skin then rests on my bottom.

"Why now?"

Ding.

The open living room is massive overlooking downtown Austin. The room is lit by the surrounding buildings and the glow from his private rooftop pool. I walk to the glass.

"Breathtaking."

"I agree." His eyes are on me.

"Dylan…" He steps closer, pulling me into his arms. "Are you sure this is wise?"

"Only one way to find out," he kisses me slow, and it leaves me trembling with need. The intimate rhythm of his tongue invades my mouth in the sweetest way, I grip the lapels of his jacket until his chest is against mine.

"Let's order dinner." I watch his eyes darken from sky blue to a vibrant hue dark enough to resemble denim.

My lips ache for a repeat , I've waited a lifetime for this moment. Before I lose my courage, I stand on my tip toes brushing my mouth against his wrapping my arms around his neck. His strong arms circle my back and lava flows through my veins to the parts that make me female.

"What do you want to eat?" His heated whisper brushes my ear, kissing my temple.

"You," escapes before I can stop it. My body aching for him to extinguish the fire he started. Not with food. But him.

"Yuki don't say it like that baby," he growls. "Dinner first. Then your gift." The promise lingering in his eyes makes the ache between my thighs intensify. He pulls me from the window to the couch. "I'll grab the menu."

I collapse on the couch.

"Make yourself at home," he says over his shoulder, loosening his tie with one hand. He walks through a door on the far end of the room. "I'll be right back."

The chant of no more Dylan is dead, its morphed into *more Dylan, please Dylan.* His kisses serve as a perfect distraction. But this is not what I need, not right now. I need to focus on getting that corner office.

I glance at the doorway hearing him move around in the back room. The open space of the living room bleeds into the dining area. Across the room, I catch a glimpse of my younger self. I walk over and see the wall lined with pictures of us over the years.

Elementary. Middle school. High school. Vacations. Each picture with Asher between us. Except one. I recognize the background, we were at Zilker Park for an outdoor concert. I am smiling at the camera, and Dylan's eyes are focused on me in the same intense gaze I saw tonight.

Has he always felt this way?

I look at the doorway anxious for his return then back at the pictures. His kisses open a hidden door I locked away years ago. A yearning I recognized for the first time our sophomore year of high school.

Asher and Dylan had a pool party at Dylan's place. As always, his parents were off traveling the world, and Momma made Asher take me along. I promised to keep quiet as long as they paid for my summer camps. But what I really wanted was a pair of diamond rings. Camps won out. They were the sensible, more affordable option, and I'd gain credits for college.

I found a spot by the pool with a book and several brochures for camps hosted around Austin, landing on a business management and entrepreneurship camp at the University of Texas. It was perfect. I circled the fee, deadline, and the website to submit my application. Satisfied I grabbed my potato chips and a Coke ready to read. Then I saw him. Really saw him.

Dylan strolled out of the house with an air of confidence that belied his fifteen years of life. Shirt off, smiling and whispering in Amber's ear. She laughed every time he leaned in, her hair blowing in the wind. I wanted more than anything to be one of the other girls.

The girls that Dylan smiled at. The girls that Dylan whispered in their ears, giving his time. To be Dylan's girl. But he didn't see me as a girl or a young woman but as Asher's sister.

Until tonight.

Continue Reading…

**Get Your Copy on Amazon
or Read in Kindle Unlimited!**

ABOUT THE AUTHOR

Ja'Nese Dixon pens tales of romance in several sub-genres. But her favorites are the ones that manage to keep readers sitting on the edge of their seats lying to themselves about reading "just one more chapter".

Ja'Nese is an avid reader and coffee drinker, who also loves to run, cook, and craft. Her ultimate goal as a writer is to give you a little "staycation" with every story. And she aims to make this present story no exception. Sit back, grab a snack and enjoy.

Ja'Nese calls Houston home with her husband, three kiddos and a four-legged diva dog.

Visit her website at www.janesedixon.com if you enjoy romance, suspense and good stories.

Subscribe to Ja'Nese Newsletter "Reader's Staycation" for reader exclusives, regular giveaways and more.

Stay in Touch:
www.janesedixon.com
info@janesedixon.com

facebook.com / AuthorJaNeseDixon

twitter.com / janesedixon

instagram.com / authorjanesedixon

amazon.com / author / janesedixon

bookbub.com / authors / ja-nese-dixon